NIGHTM

HALL PASS

Stumbling, Melissa cried out. The earth opened up and she fell in. Clumps of earth followed her, landing on her. She hit the bottom suddenly, striking something sharp which hurt.

At first she lay motionless, stunned. Then, with creeping nausea she realized... She was in a grave. Screaming, she scrambled for escape, clawing at the earth. She tore at clothing – not her clothing. Rotted fabric caught in her hands. Then hands reached down, and in her panic she grabbed them desperately, not even thinking who might be there.

"Easy," said the familiar voice. "Be quiet."

More heart-stopping Nightmares...

NIGHTMARES

HALL PASS

Robert Hawks

HarperCollins*Publishers*

First published in the USA in 1993 by Avon Books.
First published in Great Britain 1995
by HarperCollins*Publishers* Ltd.,
77-85 Fulham Palace Road, Hammersmith, London W6 8JB

1 3 5 7 9 8 6 4 2

Copyright © 1993 Robert Hawks

ISBN 0 00 675167 - 9

The author asserts the moral right to be identified
as the author of the work.

Printed and bound in Great Britain by
HarperCollins Manufacturing Ltd, Glasgow.

For Lynn
forlyn
4lyn

HALL PASS

I have no life.

Why anyone might be so arrogant as to attempt and write about a life which doesn't even exist is beyond me, beyond my grasp, beyond my understanding, beyond my comprehension. *This scrawl began as a suicide note, but having lost my nerve I now ramble on in pen about things which pain me, which I guess is the same thing as a suicide note. We all rocket forward through our lives toward death, all suffering, some more than others. Some much more than others. We all commit suicide, in our own secret, terrible ways, but almost nobody writes about why.*

Perhaps I shall.

Chapter 1

Melissa was ten feet up the hall when Holly caught up with her and said, "Hey, Mo, I hear that new guy Russell Morse is a real psycho."

Groaning, Melissa slowed and grimaced at her friend. Holly was wearing too much dark blue eye makeup and looked like a red-headed raccoon. A raccoon with an oversized shoulder bag, walking beside Melissa, trying to navigate a path to her locker. They had followed each other around since kindergarten. Both were fifteen, sophomores, but Melissa—unlike her friend—was in no particular hurry to be sixteen or a junior. "Psycho? Yeah, *right*," she said in as sarcastic a voice as she could manage. "Absolutely *everybody* in Intervention is crazy, including me. *Especially* me."

"I didn't mean that."

"You know I'm not supposed to talk about what happens down there." Intervention was a special counselling class that certain students had to take, Melissa among them. And whenever the words *special* and *certain* were used in a high school environment, nothing good could possibly follow.

Gritting her teeth, Melissa said nothing. Finally they reached her locker—number 7144—and she started spinning the ancient dial combination, 23-17-23.

Holly acted as if she had just been slugged. "Mo, I'm your best friend."

Melissa, she thought, my name is *Melissa*—Melissa Maynard—but she'd surrendered on that point years ago, along with a lot of others. Holly was a pusher, she *always* pushed, whether she was speaking up in algebra-trig class to ask a question or forcing her way through a lunchroom line. Melissa tried not to push anymore. When one pushed, people shoved right back, and sometimes they were bigger than you were. Besides, what was the hurry? The world wasn't going anywhere.

"What I heard was . . ." Holly lowered her voice to a conspiratorial whisper. "What I heard was Russell Morse killed his brother."

Rolling her eyes, Melissa snapped open the locker on the second attempt and said, "He didn't kill his brother."

Holly looked excited. "Who did he kill?"

"He didn't kill anybody."

"I heard he stabbed his brother with a pair of scissors."

"That was an accident. And he didn't kill him, he just needed some stitches."

"Yeah? So where's his brother now?"

Hardly giving it a thought, Melissa said, "Staying with relatives in Florida, I think is what I heard."

"Florida?" Holly sounded wistful. "I'd *kill* to live in Florida."

"Maybe we can get Russell to stab you too."

Frowning, Holly pulled an old copy of the Dennison school newspaper, the *Comet,* from the thick stack of debris wedged in Melissa's locker. She flipped casually through it as she spoke; the paper was a month and a half old. "Forget stab, you could just scratch me with those fingernails of yours. Sheesh, Mo, when are you going to cut those down?''

Raising her right hand, Melissa inspected her fingernails; they were nearly three quarters of an inch long and polished bright red. The product of much time and effort. "Trim my claws? Not likely . . ." They were the only part of herself of which she was really proud. Other than the nails she was just a face in the crowd: average height, average looks, average shoulder-length brown hair.

If only she had an average mind. No problems, no worries, no past. If only she could *think* before speaking sometimes. . . .

"I'm gonna leave my history book in your locker," Holly announced, half-reading still. "I don't feel like lugging it all the way back over to the main building." Dennison High consisted of three separate buildings, each ten years older than the first. The authorities, in their eternal wisdom, sometimes scheduled classes back-to-back on opposite ends of the campus. Melissa's whole day broke down like that, back and forth, back and forth. With only five minutes between bells, sometimes it seemed as if she were trying out for the track team.

"Why even ask?" The two shared lockers constantly—Holly's was located over in the auditorium building—they had each other's combinations long since committed to memory.

"I'm not asking, just telling in case I have to throw out some of your junk to make room for my books. If anything turns up missing, just check the nearest trash can."

"Uh-uh," said Melissa, pulling out stuff she needed to take to Intervention and the biology class that followed. "Love me, love my junk."

"Hey," said Holly then, just remembering. "My dad *is* going to California tonight. He's taking Mom with him, so why don't you sleep over? We can cut your hair."

"Can't."

"Your hair needs it."

"Can't sleep over. The Witch still has me on probation for that phone thing." The Witch was Melissa's stepmother of seven years. The phone thing was a minor misunderstanding from the previous summer when she accidentally ran up a two-hundred-and-seventy-dollar phone bill with a 900-number teen-talk service. Sorry hadn't been enough. Melissa spent a month wondering what the Witch wanted from her until she realized the Witch wanted nothing; she had what she wanted. Melissa was stupid, and she was now nailed down, in the lady's pocket, bingo. Toast.

Sometimes Melissa wished for parents more like Holly's; people who never seemed to be around. "How come they leave you alone so much?"

"Because they trust me."

"Trust? *You?*"

The first bell rang and Holly stuffed the newspaper back in the locker just before Melissa slammed it shut. "Sure. Why not?"

"You're the one who had the party that got raided by *three* police cars."

"Yeah," admitted Holly with a smile. "But never on a school night . . ."

Never on a school night. That's good advice, Melissa thought.

Despite appearances, Holly was good at keeping herself out of trouble. The one time she did get nailed was Melissa's fault. Melissa was—or at least Those in Authority *said* she was—a compulsive practical joker, a prankster. On the other hand, being one of the path straight and narrow, Holly was the obvious choice to be an office runner—lugging messages between the admin office and various teachers. Being her friend of ten years and very crooked, Melissa was the obvious person to corrupt her.

She gave her a note calling herself out of English class in order to get downtown and stand in line for some concert tickets.

Mistake.

Ms. McCormick, the English teacher, was more paranoid than any living being had a right to be and she released Melissa, but then checked with the office. She got an ugly response, and Melissa and Holly were both immediately nailed.

Holly pled innocent. She got two weeks of detention after school; it was her first offense.

Melissa was well known to Vice Principal Ramirez; she had a file of silliness an inch thick. Two weeks later she was assigned to Mr. Elliot's Intervention class.

Not that any of that mattered now . . .

Onward, Melissa told herself. Downstairs into the depths, but they were hardly five minutes into the Intervention discussion before Russell Morse lost his temper and broke the desk with his fist.

Not that Melissa was surprised. Being a student of human nature, she saw the explosion coming from a mile away.

First of all, Russell was late again. Last to arrive, which was appropriate since he was the newest member of the group—the last to arrive, so to speak.

First-hour Intervention had seven members, meeting in room 101 on the bottom floor of the main building. Technically eight kids were assigned but one—Janie Hoffman—didn't count because she didn't come to school anymore. Janie was a runaway; she took off from home two weeks before and nobody was really surprised, as it wasn't the first time she'd done that. Most of the kids in Intervention had run off at one time or another, and that didn't mean for an afternoon at the movies, either.

Melissa had run away herself, right after her dad got remarried; she was in third grade at the time. She managed to stay gone almost two days before being picked up by the state police—she was twenty-six miles from home.

She felt a lot farther away than that now.

As always, Melissa found herself the first to greet Mr. Elliot and take her seat in the circle, despite cutting it so close to the bell. The eight one-piece chair-desks were arranged around the counsellor's seat so that everyone could look at everyone else. Melissa sat closest to the door, watching the others arrive.

Allison Handley was next, chewing gum as always and acknowledging Mr. Elliot with barely a nod. Melissa she acknowledged not at all. Allison was a pretty girl, overweight but not quite what the cruel would consider fat. Her hair was brown, combed differently almost every day, as if she was never satisfied with what she saw in the mirror.

Gary Walden followed, a classic nerd with greasy black glasses, who quickly found his seat without meeting anyone's eyes. Then came Tracy Callahan, the music girl, who paused upon entering to surrender her purse and possessions.

Tracy lived for her music and, it seemed, little else. Failing in all of her classes, she snuck her earphones in so often that Mr. Elliot now collected the stereo from her at the door. He even took time to check what tape she had each day. " 'Kilgore Guns,' " he noted, impressed. "Are they new?"

"Very latest." Tracy was proud—she seemed to know every heavy metal band in the world. "My brother works down at Tower Records."

"These guys any good?"

7

Tracy grinned. "Anti*social.*"

That was her way of saying they were great.

Allison popped her gum throughout all of this and rolled her eyes. "That is like all so unreal."

Mr. Elliot sat the stereo on his desk and looked over. "How's that, Allison?"

"Why do you let her carry that dumb thing around school? She's like always in her own world or something—she's always bumping into people in the hall."

Mr. Elliot shrugged, greeting Tiny and Boris and shutting the door. "We do it for probably the same reason we let you chew gum in class. It's a sort of—"

"I know, I know, it's a security thing." Allison rolled her eyes again. "Gum's no big deal to me, you know. I just like to chew, you know?"

"If you don't need it, spit it out. What are you, a Bubble Yum addict?" This was from Boris, his voice as always louder than it needed to be. Small, steady, and tough, Boris was a fighter, always scuffling in the halls with somebody. His hair was crew cut and, before Russell Morse showed up, he was the kid in Intervention most likely to be shipped out to Bannerston.

Bannerston was the ultimate nightmare for an Intervention student, the reason they showed up at room 101 every morning. Bannerston was a special education facility—more like a jail—for those who just couldn't conform to discipline or a normal school. Bannerston wasn't part of the *real* world, it's where one landed when kicked out of the real world, and no matter how nice a face they tried to put on it, Intervention was the last stop before the kick.

Allison tensed, nervous. "I don't want to spit it out."

Smiling back, Mr. Elliot said, "You don't have to

spit the gum out, Allison, just try to consider other people's—''

The class door banged open then and Russell made his entrance. ''Sorry I'm late,'' he said. ''I was parking the car.''

''More like getting *run over* by a car,'' noticed Tracy. ''What happened to you?''

''Enough, enough, hold it down.'' Mr. Elliot frowned; Melissa grimaced. Russ *did* look bad. He was wearing sunglasses to cover an obviously black left eye and his lower lip was still bleeding despite the fast-food napkin he held up against it. He walked directly to the empty desk.

Mr. Elliot didn't ask *how* the injuries came about; he never asked questions like that. Instead he said, ''You look like you're prime for the nurse, Russ. Let me give you a hall pass.''

''No thanks.''

''You should get that lip looked at.''

''I think it's been attended to enough.'' Russ grinned. ''Another hall pass ain't going to change anything.'' Shaking his head Russ said, ''You guys and your notepad passes, scribbling the yeses and nos in life, the gos and no gos. Forget about it.''

''So what are you saying?''

''I'm saying I don't need a hall pass.'' Russ took his seat, settling down between Boris and Tiny. Unlike Tiny—actually a boy named James Jones, who was well over six feet tall—Russ wasn't a particularly big kid, but like Boris he wore his lousy attitude like a badge of authority. He was dressed in a Harley-Davidson motorcycle t-shirt and a black and red vest jacket, which he refused to leave in his locker. Russ carried no books, as always, just a pen, and he constantly borrowed sheets of notebook paper from people.

9

"Russ, you need to get that taken care of. You're bleeding all over yourself."

"It's nothing, don't worry about it."

Looking over, Melissa shuddered again. Russ *was* a mess.

"Russell—"

"I'm all right, I told you!" Russ slammed his fist down on his desk in a rage, and the ancient desktop shattered, splintering in three pieces from the blow. Everyone in class recoiled, Melissa especially.

"What do you want from me?" demanded Russ, standing now, juggling the broken bits of desk. "What? *What?*"

Mr. Elliot raised a calming hand. "We don't want anything from you, Russ—"

"Yeah, right. That's a bunch of crap."

Melissa half-considered jumping up and running for help, but Mr. Elliot stood his ground without even blinking. "Breaking desks isn't going to solve anything."

"No, but you know what I think sometimes?" Russ still held a long piece of splintered board from the desk.

In a flat voice Mr. Elliot asked, "What?"

"Sometimes I think you're like some psychological vampire, feeding off of us. You take, take, take. You feed off us like some leech, some vampire . . ." Russ held up the jagged piece of wood like a weapon. "Maybe I should drive this stake through your heart, Mr. Elliot. Save us all from whatever you are."

Nobody was moving; Melissa wasn't even *breathing*. They waited.

Mr. Elliot was ice. "Is that what you want to do, Russ? Kill me? Right here and now?"

Russ looked around, nervous maybe, but he didn't drop the wood. "No."

"What do you want to do?"

Russ hesitated, then shrugged. "Could we go to the library, maybe? Get out of this dungeon?"

Mr. Elliot let out a breath and a wave of relief rolled over everyone in the classroom like a wave off of the ocean. "Sure. That's a good idea. Maybe we *all* need a break. Let's do go over to the library . . ."

Chapter 2

Ms. Payne, the school librarian, seemed none too pleased as the Intervention group descended upon her, but there was no big commotion as Mr. Elliot led the class down the hall and inside the big, hollow-sounding room. They walked quietly, a tight group awaiting release. Another class was also using the library as a study hall; the kids scattered around raised their eyes as the group entered, but Melissa didn't recognize anyone.

Ms. Payne spoke with Mr. Elliot. She had red hair tied back in a tight bun and she held her hands together in front of her; Melissa remembered learning in Intervention that this was defensive body language; Ms. Payne wanted to place a barrier between herself and the person she was speaking to. Nervous, the librarian's eyes seemed very big. "Mr. Elliot, I would have *appreciated* knowing in advance that you were bringing your class down here. I could have *scheduled* something for them."

Mr. Elliot turned on the charm; he was good at that. Sometimes even Melissa felt it, and she wasn't the only one: Janie always had a big crush on him, and even Holly had been known to glide past his classroom with a wistful look on her face. Offering up a bright smile for Ms. Payne, Mr. Elliot gave her a look at *his* eyes. Bright and blue, sometimes they seemed to follow you across a room; they always seemed interested. "No need, no need for that," he said. "We're just going to enjoy some independent study time."

"Mrs. Harrison's history class is here doing research."

"That's good, that's great. I'll just keep my bunch out of their way."

Ms. Payne swallowed, wringing her hands. She nodded. "Very well."

Speaking low so as not to disturb anyone else, Mr. Elliot told everybody to relax, find something to do or read until the bell. He promised to come around to speak to each class member in turn.

Melissa grimaced. Wonderful.

No problem, she sighed; they had done this before. Tempers were like eggs and sometimes they started frying down in room 101. They had to get out somewhere: the lawn, the parking lot, the library. Melissa didn't really understand the point of all this Intervention stuff, anyway. Pseudopsychological nonsense.

There was a copy of *Glamour* magazine on the rack and Melissa grabbed it to read before taking a seat at an empty table. The Witch would probably have bought her a subscription for herself at home but she would also constantly remind Melissa about what a great person she was for giving it to her, and that was just one more thing she couldn't stomach.

There was an article on caring for long nails and Melissa started to read it, looking for tips. She didn't get too far before being interrupted.

Allison dropped her books on the reading table with a clump and pointed a finger. Allison carted more junk around with her than anyone Melissa knew; she could probably have been a weight lifter if she wanted.

13

Smacking her gum, she said, "I'm gonna leave my stuff here with you, okay?"

What was Melissa supposed to say to that? "Sure."

Allison disappeared. Melissa shoved her stuff to one side—algebra book, history book, a couple of loose-leaf notebooks, three of which were in the process of becoming "slam" books. Allison was the queen of the slam books—those stapled-together pages that asked nosy questions like *Who's the sexiest guy at Dennison?* And *Do you French kiss?* You didn't put your name under your contributions, so supposedly you could answer the questions any way you wanted, but *hours* had been spent trying to guess whose handwriting was whose. They were called slam books because if a teacher or Anybody in Authority looked as if they might catch you with one, you just slammed it shut and put an innocent look on your face.

Melissa frowned. She considered flipping through Allison's slam books, checking out what sort of dirt she was spreading now. It wouldn't be that big a deal; Allison must have started one of those a day. Still . . . Melissa figured she better not. She had enough people at this school who hated her as it was, what with one or two misguided attempts at humor.

Still . . . if Allison could be the queen of the slam books, why couldn't Melissa be the queen of the practical jokes? Certainly nobody was going to dispute the title. Melissa was, after all, the person who once greased the tile in the second-floor girl's bathroom with cooking shortening, and filled the gym shower heads with red finger-paint powder. She sent Vice Principal Ramirez's secretary Margaret a forged letter from the school board, telling her she was fired. She put rubber spiders in the cafeteria Jell-O.

It all seemed funny at the time.

Allison wasn't the only one to crowd Melissa at her

table. Tracy dropped her stuff off, and then Tiny. Boris left his stack with the growl, "Watch this junk," and Gary asked with a timid whisper, "Could you?"

Melissa sighed, nodded, and the pile grew higher. Typical library story. Nobody ever just wanted to sit with their stuff and read. Everybody wanted to prowl.

Somebody was standing above her. Melissa let her eyes flicker upward to see who was back to collect his stuff. Nobody was; it was Russ.

Wonderful.

He seemed bigger up close; Melissa sat in his shadow. He pulled off his sunglasses, and she noticed his lip had stopped bleeding. Smiling, he looked intentionally goofy, as if he knew something she didn't. Russ looked smug, like a dog who had finally nosed the lid off a trash can.

Double wonderful.

She tried not to react as he took the seat across from her. "What are you reading?" he asked, hunching over.

She showed him the cover of the magazine, hoping it might seem such a girl thing that he'd be scared off.

Russ laughed. "Wicked. Learning anything?"

Melissa shrugged. "So?"

"So? So what?"

"So what really happened to your face?"

He played with his sunglasses, but didn't put them back on. "This? Oh, this was just a minor difference of opinion with my old man."

"You got in a fight with your dad?"

"Fight? No, we don't do that anymore. We used to fight, long time ago. Now he hits, and I accept. Gracefully. It's a . . . ."

"A long story?"

"No. Just a weird one."

Melissa nodded, quiet on the inside and out.

Russ had some file folders and papers with him, and he began to sort through them. "Want to see the dirt?"

Frowning, Melissa asked, "What dirt?"

Russ showed her the name atop one of the files, typewritten on a label: *Callahan, Tracy.* Russ was grinning.

Feeling her eyes opening very wide, Melissa almost squealed. "Oh my God, those are Mr. Elliot's files."

"Sure they are. I swiped them off his desk."

"Why?"

Russ shrugged. "The guy's nuts. I always wonder what he's been writing about us. Now I'm going to find out."

"Russ, come on."

"Relax, he won't notice for a long while. Elliot's the most disorganized guy in the world. His desk is a mess, his car's a wreck. He lives in a dump."

"How would you know where he lives?"

Russ shrugged again. "I followed him home once. His place is a pit, falling apart. Total slum, I'm telling you . . ."

"You follow people home? Why?"

"He wants to know all about me, I decided I wanted to know all about *him*. Keeps us on an equal footing. Besides, no big deal, I follow lots of people home."

That scared Melissa. "You do?"

"Sure. You'd be surprised to know the neighborhoods I'm lurking around in."

The thought of Russ—or anybody like him—hiding behind the hedges as she walked home at night gave Melissa the creeps. "You shouldn't do that."

"Why not?"

"That's the kind of thing that makes people think you're dangerous."

"Really?" Russ seemed impressed. "So who thinks I'm dangerous?"

Melissa changed the subject. "Mr. Elliot is going to freak if he sees you with his files."

"Probably. Let's see what's in here . . ." Flipping through the pages, Russ found one he wanted and started to read: " 'Melissa Maynard has a troubling history of elaborate practical jokes and sick humor, bordering on compulsive behavior . . .' "

"Give me that!" Melissa dove to grab the file, but he jerked it away.

"Why? Now you're interested, eh? You want to see?"

"No, I don't want to see." But of course she did. She just didn't like the idea of Russ reading it. Who knew what might be scribbled in there about her? "How'd you get them in here?"

"Stuck them under my shirt," said Russ, very proud and confident, as if explaining how he smuggled secret military plans out of a foreign country. "I walked right out with *all* his stuff."

"You better take it back."

"Nah."

"Please . . ."

Russ looked Melissa right in the eye, curious now. "Please?"

She hesitated, then said, "Yes, please. Take the stuff back, you're going to get us all expelled or something."

Russ looked around, then back at Melissa. "You're supposed to be the big joker, what are you worried about?"

Feeling as if they were being stared at already, Melissa lowered her whisper some. "I don't want to get kicked out of school."

"Bannerston? You worried about being sent to Bannerston?"

"Yes."

Shaking his head, Russ said, "Not me. No way I'm going there." He seemed very sure of himself. "No way, no how."

"So what will you do if they try to send you?"

"Whatever I have to. Oops."

"What?"

Reacting before Melissa even saw what was happening, Russ reached over and grabbed all of the books and stuff, pulling them over on top of the files and things he had, making one big, messy pile. He adjusted her bag to cover the protruding edges of a file folder just as Mr. Elliot stepped up. "Hey, guys."

"Hi." Melissa forced a smile, fully expecting to be caught.

Russ leaned back in his chair, slipping his sunglasses over his eyes. He didn't say anything.

Mr. Elliot nodded, noticing the huge pile on the table but not recognizing what all was in it. "Looks like you guys have been appointed keepers of everybody's stuff."

"Yeah," said Russ. "Well, somebody has to do it."

Mr. Elliot turned to Melissa. "How you doing today, Ms. Maynard?"

"Fine. Great." *We're nailed*, Melissa thought, *I know we're nailed.*

"I see you signed up for driver's ed."

"Yeah," she said, rolling her eyes. "I signed up, but there's no way I'll get in."

Driver's education was offered to sophomores. They could sign up to take it one semester instead of study hall, but they still had to be approved by the vice principal's office. In her case, Melissa thought that unlikely. They'd be afraid of what she might do to the cars. Besides, her study hour was already taken up by Intervention.

"You might be surprised," said Mr. Elliot.

"I doubt it," she said. Driver's ed was a ticket out of Intervention. If you made it through a semester without it, why would they send you back?

"I don't know. Janie was set to go to driver's ed."

This was a surprise. "She was?"

There *was* hope. Janie was the Intervention student who ran away from home, and if she could get picked for driver's ed, anybody could. Melissa could.

"Hey, Mr. E., how's your house coming along?" Russ gave her a half-wink as he interrupted with this question and she had to keep herself from cringing.

Mr. Elliot stared at Russ a moment; something passed between them, but then he laughed. "The old-fixer-upper, you mean? She'll be a real winner when we get around to actually doing some things, but I have to admit I never seem to find the time. The windows sag, the floors creak, I guess I'm lucky the roof hasn't fallen in on me yet. Good thing the neighborhood's no better."

"Yeah," said Russ. "Good old Vanzetti." The Vanzetti was the name of a bad part of town, the same part Russ lived in.

"You volunteering to come by and help out?" Mr. Elliot's smile was teasing.

Russ grimaced. "Ah, I don't know, Mr. E., physical labor and me don't get along so well; you know that. I'm more executive material."

"Might do you some good."

"Mr. Elliot, *please* . . ." Ms. Payne's whisper sounded almost desperate.

"Sorry." Holding up a hand in apology, Mr. Elliot

19

nodded at Melissa and Russ again. "Gotta go. See you guys on Monday."

Russ watched him walk over to somebody else's table. "What a loser."

Melissa took a deep breath. "We're lucky he didn't see his stuff under all the others."

Russ shook his head, repeating himself. "He's a *loser*. He must be. Why else do you think they stuck him with the crazy kids?"

That made Melissa mad. She looked Russ right in the eye. *"I'm* not crazy."

Russ smiled back. "Sure you're not."

Before she could say anything else the bell rang. Allison and the others rushed back and for a moment there was a tangle for belongings, then everyone seemed to just disappear around Melissa, as did most everything off of the table, including her pencils and the *Glamour* magazine she was reading.

"Absolutely terrific," Melissa said to herself. Readying to leave the library, she pulled her stuff together. She wanted to chase after Russ, find out what he was going to do, but at the same time she knew she should put nothing but distance between her and anybody like him.

So she did. But still she wondered: What was in her file? Was he going to return them? What was he going to see? What might he learn about her that she didn't even know about herself?

Wonderful thoughts, all.

On to algebra-trig class, the hour of the day that went most slowly, Fridays especially. Melissa was late, as always. Mrs. Hegg was already writing page and problem numbers on the blackboard. She'll give me a tardy slip later, Melissa thought. Headache time.

She stuffed things under her seat and opened up

20

her notebook for a sheet of paper to write on, but the page was full, as were most of them. Melissa realized right away that it wasn't her notebook. It had a blue cover, and was straight out of the student store, but it wasn't hers. In the pile-up on the library table she had wound up with somebody else's notebook.

Terrific. No great tragedy, Melissa supposed, but it was a pain. Whose notebook was it? There wasn't any name and she didn't recognize the handwriting. Hand *printing*, actually. It looked like poetry. Or a diary, maybe . . .

I am a fly on the wall, said the writer, whom Melissa still couldn't identify. *I can see myself, it's as if I am two different halves of one person. I don't know who I am. And maybe I'll find out too late.*

Whose handwriting was this? It was almost a scrawl, as though written by the fingers of a broken hand. Melissa flipped through. The notebook was full of lots of sarcastic, gossipy comments, the writer's private notes to himself. A lot of gripes about how whiny everybody in Intervention seemed, and it almost made Melissa laugh because she agreed. Was this one of Allison's slam books? That made no sense. Who in the class did she like enough to share thoughts with?

Tiny barfed today, said one page. *I think he eats chili dogs for breakfast.*

I remember that, Melissa thought, catching herself in mid-giggle. That happened a few months ago, right in class. She realized a lot of the notebook was a diary. Immediately she felt guilty, but she read at the same time. This was great stuff.

Totally ignoring the assignment on the board, Melissa flipped through the pages, curious, when suddenly she stopped, no longer breathing. The words she saw now burned a hole right into her brain.

I had to kill Janie, it said. *She said she could*

keep the secret, but she lied, she was going to tell, going to tell and that can't happen, not now, not yet.

Although I cried my eyes out after, I was really surprised.

There was hardly any blood.

Chapter 3

It's a joke.

Melissa almost laughed with relief when she realized it had to be, all the notebook stuff. Mrs. Hegg flashed her a cold stare and Melissa stuffed the incriminating thing away, doing her best to look like she was paying attention to the scribbles on the blackboard.

A joke. Yes, that made perfect sense. There was nothing wrong with having a sick sense of humor. Melissa's own laughs aimed toward the dark side. But . . .

But Janie was gone, right? She was missing.

Of *course* she was missing. Sheesh, it wouldn't make much sense to write in a dummied-up notebook that you've killed somebody whom you see everyday. That would really be weird. You have to pick a target that's gone, a person who might very well have been viciously murdered. That's where you stake your claim, that's the blood you call your own, that's the joke, the . . . uh . . .

Sick sense of humor or not, Melissa had to pause for thought: What was so funny about that?

Not much.

So what was the point?

Cheap shot. The point was that there was no point.

23

Melissa of all people knew that; it was the essence of the practical joke—a few moments of pointless viciousness, with an edge, followed by laughter. If some third party didn't get the joke, then, well, too bad, so sad. That was life in the fast lane.

So it didn't matter if Melissa didn't get the intended joke, because God knew there were dozens of pranks she had pulled off in her time that caused lots of grief and seemed to amuse no one. No one but Melissa. And some of those didn't even seem funny to her anymore. Did that make her sick? Or crazy?

Maybe. She was in Intervention, after all, and if Mr. Elliot had passed along any bits of wisdom at all it was this—everything means something. . . .

Mrs. Hegg presented her with a yellow tardy slip on her way out the door and Melissa frowned, tucking it inside her algebra book. Another detention coming; add it to the pile. There were worse things in life.

Holly grabbed Melissa by her locker again, this time with news of Teddy Wallace.

Obviously distracted, Melissa was still flipping through the pages of the mysterious notebook. Holly jumped right in and snatched it away from her—Holly was always snatching things. "What's this? Writing a book?"

Melissa shrugged. She didn't bother to try and grab it back; such a struggle was pointless. She said, "It's a notebook, somebody's diary, I think. I found it after library today."

"Library? When do you have library?"

"Intervention library, okay? I've got somebody's notebook and now I don't have a clue what to do with it."

"Sell it."

"Holly, please."

"Burn it."

"I can't do that."

"Sell it, burn it, do something. You sure don't need any more problems, such as getting caught with somebody else's stuff again."

Melissa ignored the advice. She took the notebook back and stuffed it on her top locker shelf, saying to Holly, "Okay, what problems trouble you now?"

"I just told you. *Teddy.*"

The name rang a bell. "The sax player? Guy in the band?"

"Guy with his *own* band. Gorgeous with an attitude."

"Terrific. And?"

"I've got him coming over tonight."

"So wonderful for you."

"Mo, come on. Now you have to sleep over, I can't have him at the house without somebody around."

"Why not?" It was a valid question, because Melissa knew that Holly did one thing better than anyone else in the whole world, and that included any other planets where people might live and utter sounds. What Holly did best was talk to guys.

It was a gift. Melissa herself fell into that massive category of people whose tongues turned to thick rubber and brains turned to birdseed whenever confronted with a smiling member of the opposite sex.

Holly had no secrets to pass along, nothing you could learn by watching her in action, anyway, and her advice on the subject was absolutely useless. "Be yourself," she said.

Right. Herself was the last person Melissa wanted to be when in the presence of a guy. Julia Roberts, maybe. Miss February, perhaps. But herself? Hardly.

Story of her life. All of her talents and good qualities were deep dark secrets she would take to the grave, while her faults and all the bad stuff was right there in the window for the world to see.

It was easy to talk about loneliness, but teaching it to yourself was something beyond description. That deep bone-aching that you don't understand yourself until it settles in as a sickness, sapping your strength. Soft, Melissa was, but some of that softness came from the ache, the coolness. Loneliness wasn't cold, it wasn't a shock, a freeze that took you in the night; it was cool, something that crept like consumption. It made you stay home, and eventually made you stay in one corner of a room, one bit of furniture, searching out one place in the world where it didn't hurt to think about things.

Melissa just wanted to be warm.

It was like the jokes she pulled off on people. They weren't mean-spirited, or at least she didn't intend them that way. Real life was just never as exciting or as funny as the things that popped into her head, and Melissa wanted people to like her, not to be totally bored by her.

Which brought up the next question, because Holly had also mastered the extension of the art—talking to guys without any other people—moral support—standing behind her. So Melissa asked, "What do you need me there for?"

"Backup."

"Backup? What are you going to do? Mug him?"

"Come on, Mo, be serious."

"I'm always serious," said Melissa, and, even as she said it, she realized it was getting to be more and more true. The days of the carefree practical joker, the caution-to-the-wind girl were over, or at least she hoped they were. Nothing good ever really came from any of it, and the grief she lugged around in buckets.

"You're still not answering."

"I've answered six times, Holly, you just never hear until you get the answer you want."

Holly's smile was bright. "Call it a pleasant personality defect. Come on, if the old man finds out I had some guy over by his lonesome while they were out of town my life will be officially over."

Melissa sighed. "I'll ask the Witch, okay? That's all I can do."

"Good. It also might help if you don't actually call her the Witch. Try 'Mom.' "

"She's not my mother."

"Okay, so how about Jeanette? That is her name."

"I know her name."

"Courtesy is contagious, Mo."

"So you keep saying."

Holly frowned.

Melissa surrendered. "I'll give it my best shot."

Immediately pleased, Holly smiled. "Good. Because I think Teddy's bringing along somebody for you."

Melissa stopped cold, looking at her friend. "You told me you weren't going to do that anymore."

Bells were ringing; Holly ducked the question by shrieking, "I'm late! I'm too far away! I'm doomed!"

"Holly!"

Holly was already taking off. "Later," she said. "I gotta run! See you at lunch!"

Melissa did see Holly at lunch, in the cafeteria. Melissa had two tardy slips now, and plenty of gripes about Holly, but she had no luck in talking her out of another attempt at fixing her up with yet another guy. The most Holly would promise was, "Relax, this time it'll be wonderful, this time it'll be great."

Great. Right. More empty promises from Holly. Melissa was so distracted by this nonsense she virtually forgot about the scary stuff in the notebook; she

27

left it in her locker at school, more worried about the ugly evening ahead.

Holly had another of her many clubs after school, so Melissa walked home alone, with no chance to debate things. Holly usually had some sort of meeting—drama club, Spanish club, audio-visual club, and some weird school pep thing called R.T. It was a wonder she had any time left for guys, much less those added minutes needed to intrude into Melissa's private life.

A joke, she thought, the situation absolutely calls for a joke of some kind, some sort of a trap for this Teddy and his uninvited friend. Something quick, cruel, and funny; something to put them in their place. Melissa's first thought was to really scag it up, grease her hair up with gel, get it thick and matted so it looked filthy. She could wear grungy-looking clothes and mismatched socks. Heck, mismatched shoes, one of them green. Show up for this unasked-for private party looking and acting like the blind date from hell. Spend the night giggling like a fool and trying to kiss Teddy's poor friend; send him screaming from the house. Holly would love that one.

Mean, vicious thoughts, girl. Unacceptable, remember? With a sigh, Melissa tried to adjust her thinking. That was the big Intervention thing, wasn't it? Another of Mr. Elliot's great life lessons? In times of stress, try and adjust your thinking. Holly meant well, after all; she was trying to be a friend. It was time for Melissa to play nice.

Walking home, Melissa tried to keep her mind on things that mattered. Her stepmother had left her a note that morning, instructions to bring home bread and milk, so she was going to stop at Terry's.

Terry the Terror ran the Texaco station on the corner of Edgemont and Franklin streets. To be honest, the place was a microwave burrito and soda store that sold a little gasoline on the side, and it was a total kid hangout, despite Terry's occasional blowups. In his mid-thirties, Terry had a Fu Manchu mustache, a short temper, and a mission in life—the sole purpose of which was rebuilding a 1968 Mustang he struggled with during his spare moments at the station, and a few teenage motorheads scored a lot of brownie points by helping him out evenings and weekends.

Curt McLaughlin was one of them Melissa knew; he always seemed to be knee-deep in grease and oil, but Curt wasn't all motorhead. He sat across from Melissa and Holly in history, and answered a lot of the questions Mr. Anderson would toss out at the class. Curt seemed to like history. History and cars. Weird.

Crossing the parking lot past the great monument of the Mustang, Melissa cut toward the store entrance. Seeing Curt standing above the open car hood, she gave him a wave. That was when a familiar-sounding voice shouted, "Retribution!" Russell Morse came racing out from behind the back of the garage, cradling something in his hand. Melissa found out too late what it was—a grease gun of some sort, which he held out in front of him now.

Curt ducked out of blind instinct, and when Russell got off the squirt of grease it flew past Curt and splattered Melissa.

Oh God, she thought, jumping back, but it was too late. Specks of slimy grease covered the front of her blouse and her purse and her books. She wiped at her chin with the back of her hand, but the grease seemed to have missed her face. Wonderful.

Russell grimaced, at first holding it back, but then he laughed outright. "Oops."

Melissa considered throwing her greasy books across the car at him. "It's not funny."

29

"It is. It's a little funny."

No wonder people hated Russell. No wonder they thought he was a punk. He *was* a punk. Definitely.

Terry the Terror was there now, out of the garage and yelling. He grabbed the grease gun from Russell and slapped him hard on the back, calling him a few choice names. Russell was another of the guys who put in time helping out, but now Terry was shouting, "Out of here, get out of here. I don't want to see you back."

Russell wasn't exactly broken up; he just shrugged. "Great, do me another favor."

"Get walking."

"I was aiming for Curt, he's got me before."

"Out, you're out of here."

Russell sneered. "Fine. Who cares?" He took off down the street; Melissa watched as he disappeared around the corner.

Curt tried to help, rushing over and saying, "Hey, Mo. Melissa, I'm sorry, are you okay?"

Melissa hesitated, turning. She had to brush the hair from her eyes. *Okay*. There was a word that covered a lot of ground. If you were in an airplane crash from thirty thousand feet and walk away with broken bones and burns, you're considered a survivor. You are okay. If you trip going upstairs to play Nintendo and get a bloody nose, you are not okay. In which category did getting splattered with grease fall?

"Sheesh, I'm sorry . . ." He started to reach out to her with an already soiled orange rag; Melissa backed out of his reach.

"It's all right," she said, "You'll just spread it around. I'll get it later."

"Will that stuff come out?"

"I don't know. I hope so."

Curt nodded. "If it doesn't I'll buy you another blouse. I mean I'll give you money. I mean . . ."

30

"It's all right, I just want to get out of here."

Another nod from Curt; he seemed desperate for something else to say. "Headed home?" he asked.

"No choice." Especially now, she thought.

Curt's third nod. He was wiping his hands on the rag now. "Are you going to be in trouble?"

Melissa thought about it. "Oh, only more trouble than you could ever dream of . . ."

The old man is calling me.

He's been dead a long time now, my father. Cremated. I can't even romance about decaying bones, or disturbances reaching him even unto the grave, because there is no grave. His ashes aren't even scattered, they're held in a communal something or other. All I know is it meant not having to suffer some horror of carting him about, or emptying his remains into a public ashtray. Fitting as that might have been, it would have meant the end of me.

Still, he calls. Mostly in dreams, if you believe in those sorts of things. Most likely just another jagged piece of my sanity shearing free.

Having never read much Kipling, I have to accept as true (from the movie version) that as the Indian water bearer dragged himself through hostile fire to climb the steps of the Temple of Gold, the colonial British officer murmured, "You are a better man than I, Gunga Din."

Anyway, I hope it is true.

Chapter 4

Melissa's stepmother was arguing with the dogs when she got home. Sneaking in the back way, Melissa heard Jeanette in the front room, threatening Skeeter and Bingle with ugly-sounding dog punishments.

The hounds better look sharp, thought Melissa as she closed the back door behind her. Jeanette always followed through on her threats.

Melissa tried to plot a course. There was no way upstairs, or to the laundry room, without getting past Jeanette. And Jeanette was never going to let this grease thing slide without comment. More than comment; verbal assault. Maybe even a few ugly-sounding punishment threats, as if her stepdaughter were just one of the dogs.

Melissa found herself making a fist. One of these days, she thought, one of these days . . .

Take a breath, girl, take a breath. Melissa gave herself strict instructions. Remember Intervention, remember Mr. Elliot. There's always a reason to think things through. There's always a reason to think, period.

Just aim yourself upstairs. Get out of sight and in your room. Don't make such a big deal out of things. Go on . . .

She didn't get far, though. She didn't get far because Jeanette came into the kitchen, saw her standing there by the breakfast nook, and did a double take. Stopping dead in her tracks, Jeanette sort of rolled her eyes upon seeing Melissa and the state she was in. "Okay. So what happened?"

It never even occurred to Melissa to just answer. Her first thought was desperate: *Quick. Story.* Something that will fly.

Melissa sighed. "Just an accident."

Unimpressed, Jeanette's eyes were cruel. "A joke, you mean?"

"No, it was just something outside Terry's—"

"Enough!"

Melissa jumped, waited.

Scratching at her head, Jeanette said—for probably the millionth time—"What is the point of all these lies?"

"It's . . . it's not a lie . . ."

"It's *totally* a lie. You've ruined another good blouse, God knows how, and you walk in ready to spout off another one of your fairy tales."

"Sorry."

"No. No, I don't think you are sorry. Not one little bit."

Melissa shouldn't have said anything, didn't mean to, tried not to, but before she could grab the words and toss them back she heard herself acknowledging, "No, I'm probably not."

Jeanette didn't explode, she was calm and quiet. The worst possible combination. She opened the refrigerator and said, "Get the dogs outside."

"What?"

"You heard me."

"They're not *my* dogs."

"Do it; you're already filthy anyway."

Terrific, thought Melissa. Wonderful. The amazing things she brought on herself by never knowing when

34

to shut up. The dogs were no fun to mess with at all; Skeeter and Bingle had no sense of logic. First they fought to stay outside, then they fought to stay inside. Not to mention that they were unusually big dogs, half-dalmation and half-dinosaur, Melissa sometimes thought, and they knew every dog trick in the book, like limping after you spanked them just to make you feel guilty. They slobbered on you, they wrestled, they snapped and bit; trying to get them to do anything was a nightmare.

Of course, compared to arguing with Jeanette the Witch, fighting the dogs was a picnic. "Okay, all right," said Melissa. "I'll get them out. They listen to me sometimes."

Jeanette said nothing. Rummaging through the cabinets, she started pulling things out for dinner.

Melissa swallowed, dived right in. "I do need to go out tonight . . ."

"You're grounded. "Jeanette said it so coldly, so finally, as if it were a death sentence beyond appeal.

Melissa gave it her best shot. "Yeah, I know, but this isn't really for me. It's—"

"I don't care what it is."

"I *know* you don't.

"Don't push it."

Very frustrated, Melissa said, "Come on, Holly's having some big problems today. She needs to talk to me."

"Not while you're grounded."

"She's my friend, she's my responsibility . . ."

"It's really hard to listen about how responsible you are when you're standing there in an expensive blouse covered with motor oil."

"That was an accident."

"Which doesn't really matter, not after you went to all the trouble to try and lie about it."

"Why not lie?" Melissa felt half-crazy even talk-

35

ing about it. "You never listen to me when I tell the truth."

Glaring, Jeanette said, "Don't give me that. Your father and I listen too much; that's why you have so many problems. You try and get over, even when you don't. I can't get him to realize that, and I don't understand you at all."

"You don't understand too much."

Jeanette shook her head. "Forget it; I don't even want to look at you. Get on up to your room."

Realizing that she'd pushed too far, Melissa tried to back off. "Come on, Jeanette, give me a break."

"You heard me."

"Come on, Jeanette, that's always your answer, isn't it? Send me off, get me out of the way. That's always the easy way out, isn't it? You—"

Ring! Ring!

Melissa grimaced. The phone was ringing. She didn't grab for it, but Jeanette nodded, walked slowly over to the kitchen extension, and picked it up. Jeanette answered, listened for a moment, then frowned, holding up the white receiver. "It's for you."

Melissa sighed and walked over to the telephone. She had to; she was no longer allowed a phone in her room. Yet another repercussion from the 900-number phone bill. Taking the receiver, she said, "Hello?"

"Hello, Mo." Holly's singsong voice. She was up to something.

"What?"

"Oh, aren't we snotty today?"

"Guess why." Melissa spoke through clenched teeth.

"You bring it all on yourself," said Holly. "I don't feel the least bit sorry for you."

"I'm crushed." Melissa was waiting for the Witch to leave the kitchen, so she could explain, but Jeanette just puttered around, pretending like she had things to do. Disgusting.

Unaware of all this, Holly said, "Well, your great mystery is solved. I know who wrote your weird notebook thing."

"What notebook thing?"

"I've got that notebook. The one you were talking about at school."

It took Melissa a second to realize what Holly was talking about. First she was surprised, and then she was angry. *"You've* got it? How did you get it?"

"From your locker. You made it sound so juicy I grabbed it to read in study hall. I didn't think you'd care. Then I got so into it I brought it home with me."

"Holly!"

"Listen, this is great stuff."

"I'm so sure."

"It's all about you guys, all you guys, the Intervention kids, there's a lot of stuff about *you* in it. *Weird* stuff."

Melissa started to bite her lip. She was embarrassed and she was upset and she was angry all at the same time. Okay, so the notebook had a sick joke or two in it, okay, but Melissa hadn't really read too much of it, but she had read enough to know she didn't like the idea of Holly going over the thing line by line. Who knew what might be in there? "Intervention is supposed to be private."

"Apparently not *too* private."

"You shouldn't be reading that," Melissa said, but what she was thinking was *Stop it, Holly, just stop it.*

Holly sniffed. "Who are you to give lectures? You're the one who snatched it in the first place."

"That was a mistake."

"So why didn't you give it back?"

"I didn't know who to give it back to. Besides . . ."

37

"Besides what?"

Melissa hesitated, not knowing exactly what to say. She skirted the issue with a question. "How much did you read?"

"I told you, a lot. It gets better every page."

"Did you read anything, uh, scary, maybe?"

"The whole thing's scary. This guy's a nut."

"It's a guy?" That would answer one question.

"Maybe. Maybe a guy, maybe a girl. I'm not telling until you come over."

"I can't. How did you figure out whose notebook it is?"

"Through my special brand of great deductive reasoning. That plus the fact that I know how guys think, and once you know how they think it isn't hard to tell one from another."

"So what do you know?"

"Well, I haven't read it all, but so far there's enough gooshy stuff here to get somebody tossed in the funny farm. We're going to have a good time with this, Mo."

"I don't want to have a good time with this."

"You will, trust me. Remember the fairy-tale story of Rumpelstiltskin?"

"The fairy tale? I guess so."

"This bad troll demon was going to steal the princess's baby, and the only way to beat the guy was to figure out his name."

"Yeah?"

"Yeah. So when you get over here tonight I'll tell you who I think Rumpelstiltskin is." Holly giggled, very pleased with herself. "You are definitely going to like the answer."

Watching Jeanette, Melissa turned to the wall and spoke low into the phone again. "I can't come. I told you. Just tell me."

"Sneak out."

"Holly!"

"You've done it before; I need you over here."

"I can't."

"We can all read the notebook together."

Rolling her eyes, Melissa said, "Holly . . ."

"I'm telling you, this notebook is gooshy stuff. This person is *crazy*. They'll give us *anything* to get it back. We'll *own* them."

"Yeah?" Melissa swallowed. "Crazy funny, or crazy *crazy?*" Melissa was thinking of the lines she'd read, deep in the middle of the thing. The sick joke about killing Janie. *If it was a joke . . .*

Forget that thought.

"Crazy *crazy,*" said Holly. "It'll be good enough. We'll get over."

"Get over on who?"

Holly sort of shrugged the whole thing off. "I don't know, I'm not telling. And if you don't come over maybe I'll just read it to the guys. I'm halfway through, anyway."

For no reason at all, the idea of Holly finishing the notebook suddenly scared Melissa. *Why?* It wasn't anything she could explain, but suddenly those words *I killed Janie* were there, right in front of her eyes, and she wanted to scream into the phone, shout out a warning for Holly not to read anymore.

Crazy. That really *would* sound crazy. So, instead of sounding crazy, Melissa tried to sound irritated. "Well, like I said, you shouldn't be reading that stuff." Melissa really felt a bit of the anger she was trying to project. The idea of catching a glimpse of somebody's notebook diary was one thing, but flipping through the thing like it was a public slam book was a completely different ball of wax. Or was she only thinking that way because she was written about in it?

Good question. Melissa had to consider that one.

After all, she was the practical joker, the one who liked to put others on the spot, leave others hanging in the wind, in uncomfortable situations.

Time to sigh.

Because Melissa had to face up to the obvious. If not for her name being mentioned in the thing, she probably could have easily rationalized making photocopies and leaving incriminating pages of the notebook all over the cafeteria.

But that wasn't what was suddenly scaring her, suddenly making her think crazy thoughts. It made no sense, but it was as if the notebook was something contaminated, something somehow dangerous. Something that could be disposed of, tossed away if one acted quickly enough, but never unread, not once the words were in your brain.

It was a line Melissa was conscious of having come across somewhere, she didn't remember exactly; some horror novel probably. *Once thou hath rolled back the stone, the time to make blind thy sight is done and lost.*

For you have looked the devil in the eye, and you are his.

Chapter 5

As always, Melissa was not quite ready for school Monday morning, but the government and parents had laws and you either obeyed or took your lumps. Melissa knew all about that; she had been lumped before. Melissa's father, Tony Maynard, was already at the kitchen table when she trudged downstairs. He was eating a steak and some french fries, both buried in more ketchup than most humans confront in a lifetime.

Melissa's father worked for the post office, but he worked the graveyard shift, supervising the guys routing and trucking mail in and out in the dead of night. He loved his job, but his body clock was totally turned inside out and upside down, and when Melissa's day was starting, his was winding down.

Which was probably for the best. The less she had to explain about her life, the better, although a lot of times her father was her only ally in the Great War Against the World, and she missed not having more time to talk to him. Especially since the arrival of Jeanette the Witch.

Melissa made two quick pieces of toast and nibbled at one while she poured a glass of water. She spoke first, saying, "Holly's probably furious at me."

Looking up from his last few bites of steak, her father chewed, swallowed, and asked, "Why now?"

"She wanted me to sneak out Friday night."

This remark drew a thoughtful nod. "So did you?"

"Sneak out? No way. She wanted me to come sleep over."

"And party with some guys."

"Of course." That was the difference between Melissa's talking to her father and talking to her stepmother. With Dad she could at least be honest. Had she said the same thing to Jeanette the Witch, a loud tirade against Holly would have already begun.

The old proverb was wrong. Honesty was hardly ever the right policy.

Another nod from Dad. "Well, I appreciate the thought. And I'll talk to Jeanette. This grounding's about due to be over with anyway."

"Thanks." Melissa didn't really want to say anymore, but she had to, because she was wary. "You won't let her talk you out of it."

"Missy . . ." Dad always called her Missy when he felt himself boxed in a corner.

"She's always preaching against me."

"She doesn't preach against you."

"She does. She says a bunch of bad stuff and you wind up on her side."

"Missy . . ."

"I feel like we're caught between some things. I'm always alone with her, you're never here."

Her father hesitated, because he knew it was more true than not, although he would never admit to the fact. What he said was, "I think I can make up my own mind and keep it for a while. Will you trust me?"

Melissa swallowed and nodded. Give it another chance.

Dad gave another nod. "So how's school going?"

Melissa shrugged. "Uneventful."

Dad took a sip of his coffee. "And this Intervention thing, what about that? Is it working out all right?"

"It's all right. It's not terrible, I mean. I'd still rather be in driver's ed."

"Maybe next term."

Fat chance, thought Melissa, as always. But she didn't say this. Not to her father.

He was just about ready to settle himself in the living room, in front of the TV. The couch from which he would greet Jeanette when she made her way down, and where he'd fall asleep for a short nap before dragging himself upstairs for a longer sleep. Taking her second piece of toast, Melissa grabbed her books and gave him a wave good-bye. Time to start hoofing it to school.

The day was bright and cheerful and that was good. The October air was cool and Melissa felt better. In the light of day, it wasn't hard to figure out why she felt better. Come on, she told herself, the whole notebook thing wasn't that big a deal. At worst it was a joke—a joke on her. And now that she understood, she felt better because she wasn't about to fall for any nonsense.

Not today, anyway.

One weird thing, Holly wasn't home when Melissa stopped by to meet her for the walk to school; at least, there was no answer at the door, and she stood there rapping for a while. Frowning, Melissa checked her watch and walked on by herself, expecting to find Holly around each corner, waiting and wondering if Holly was even going to be at school when she got there.

Melissa took the Vanzetti shortcut, which you could do during the daylight hours, if you walked fast and had the nerve.

The Vanzetti, called that because of a once powerful but long-dead family that owned so much of the property, was an old neighborhood, having been in disrepair for as long as Melissa could remember. Graying paint chipped and peeled, grass died, and only the October wind bothered with arrangements for the leaves scattered about beneath gnarled trees.

No real families remained in this neighborhood; the rich were long gone and the truly destitute could not yet afford to collect here. People died here. The neighborhood was like a poisoned water hole on the African veldt, gathering dregs of herds who found themselves too weary to move on.

Melissa snapped up her step. She didn't like to linger while passing through the Vanzetti, especially when she was walking alone. Besides, she didn't want to be late.

Holly was never late.

Come on, that wasn't true. Everybody was late for school sometimes, and getting worked up was pointless. So Holly had left without her, no big deal.

Most likely it was no big deal.

Melissa had a hard time convincing herself on that, though, and she wasted a lot of time looking around and asking different people if they had seen Holly. Nobody had.

So don't worry about it. This isn't any big deal, this isn't any real big deal.

And in the end it wasn't a big deal. There she was now, Holly, and still a couple minutes to go before the bell. Melissa saw Holly coming down the hall, but she seemed a little spooked as she hurried over. "I need to talk to you."

Knowing full well what was coming, Melissa tried to cut her off, kill the issue right away. She talked quickly as she spun her locker combination, not letting Holly sneak a word in. "Look, I couldn't get

44

out. The Witch was watching me all weekend, she even made me bake with her. She likes the idea of that, me baking cookies. Cookies build character, I guess. I'm just about ungrounded and she's looking for anything she can to nail me with, so if she wants me to bake cookies I have to bake cookies.''

Holly shook her head. ''Who cares about cookies? I've got to talk to you about this notebook.''

''Yeah. I—''

Melissa stopped talking, momentarily stunned speechless. She had just pulled open her locker and it was a wreck, a mess.

Oh, *terrific* . . .

''Wow.'' Holly couldn't help but comment on it.

Melissa's locker was trashed, *again*. All the books had been pulled down to where she usually hung her coat, and they were open, some pages ripped, others probably missing. Melissa had a cat calendar, which hung from the locker door; that was gone, or at the very least somewhere in that thick pile of torn and wadded papers.

Wonderful. Disgusted, she started to pull things together.

Holly was quiet. ''Oh, no.''

''Oh, yeah.''

''You should tell the office.''

''Why?'' There was no point in bothering to report it, the same thing happened every year, it seemed. Aggravated, Melissa flipped around some more, suddenly worried. ''Where's the sweater?''

''What?''

''The sweater. The Witch's white lace thing, which I wasn't supposed to borrow, but I did.''

''I thought you took it home.''

''No, I was hiding it in here.'' Melissa couldn't help closing her eyes a second. *Dig the hole,* she thought. *I'm dead.* Frustrated, she opened her eyes

45

and asked Holly, "Did you leave my combination lying around for somebody to find?"

"*No*. I don't even have it written down." Holly was thinking. "I bet I know who did this, though."

"My life is over and I can't find my history book. My homework was in there."

"Oh, God, I bet I *do* know."

Finally hearing what Holly was saying, Melissa asked, "Who?"

"I can't tell you."

"Terrific. Now which one of us is acting crazy?"

"I'm *serious*. I think the person who wrote this notebook knows you've got it."

"Great, they know and you know. When do you fill me in?"

Holly shook her head, suddenly confident. "No, I've got this figured out. It's better you don't know. That way you can't get in trouble."

"I'm already in trouble."

"No. Trust me. I can't tell you now."

"Right, Holly. Sorry. I figured it out, and I'm not falling for it."

"Figured what out?"

"The game. This is all just a game."

"A game?"

"Yeah," said Melissa, as if it were all so obvious. "I do jokes and now somebody else is playing a game. Maybe it's you."

"Me? I think not."

"Well, somebody is. This is like some big, gross movie on notebook paper."

Holly considered this. "I wish it was. I mean, I hope you're right. I hope it is a game." She thought another second, something new occurring to her. "I guess it could be, considering who was writing it."

"So what did you read?" asked Melissa. "Did you read about Janie?"

"Yeah. Did you?"

"Just part of it."

The warning bell was ringing; two short bursts. Ninety seconds to get to class. The halls started emptying.

Melissa gave up on the mess in her locker, grabbed a few books, and said, "I've got to go."

Holly acted like she was startled. "You mean you're just going to go down there? To Intervention?"

"What else am I supposed to do?"

"Well, what I mean is—"

"You won't even tell me what you know."

"Yeah, but for all you know there's a dangerous person down there."

"Start passing out knives and we're all dangerous."

"Come on, let's ditch and look at this thing."

Melissa was shocked. "You want to ditch? *You?* The great cheerleader Holly?"

Insulted, Holly said, "This is scary, weird stuff I'm talking about here. And this isn't the place to talk about it."

Any second the final bell was going to ring. Any second. Melissa felt that minor panic starting to set in her stomach, that fear of "getting in trouble" that everyone seemed to work so hard to drill into her. Melissa said, "I can't ditch right now. Let's talk about it at lunch."

Bam! At that moment the locker slammed shut, pushed by a grinning Russell Morse, and both girls jumped. Russell still wore sunglasses to cover his black left eye, but his lower lip was now scabbed over. He was wearing the same black and red vest jacket as always, now speckled brown in spots. Yesterday's bloodstains. Melissa wondered if that was supposed to be some macho statement or something.

47

Holly stopped talking and Russ laughed, saying, "Hey, ladies, we're all late together."

He was right. The final bell was ringing overhead. The halls were nearly empty.

Melissa felt her stomach go tight. Terrific.

Russ nudged her, as if he was in on a joke or something. "Hey, grease girl, how's it going?"

Grimacing, Melissa said, "Oh, yeah. Thanks for getting me in so much trouble."

"I was shooting for Curt. He's the one who needed to be slicked up."

"Yeah, well, thanks for nothing."

Russ seemed genuinely shocked. "You got in trouble? Really?"

"Absolutely."

"Sorry." So much for guilt, he was on to the next subject. "You going to psycho*mania* today?"

Russ had one of those smart-aleck grins that made you want to just reach over and smack him across the face, make him drop it, make him wake up to the real world.

Or maybe not.

Melissa answered. "Yeah, I'm going."

Russ wouldn't drop the smirk. He said, "We're oh so very late."

"It's okay," said Melissa, moving away from Holly and leaving it up to Russ to follow if he wanted. "I've been late before . . ."

Chapter 6

"I told you guys we should have locked the door."

This was from Allison Handley, making a wise-crack when Melissa pushed her way into room 101, followed by Russ, who sort of ambled his way through the door. This in itself produced a series of "Oooh," noises from the various juvenile dweebs in the room, and Melissa realized with some embarrassment that her biggest panic right now was the fear that everyone would assume she and Russ were together.

They were together, but they weren't together *together*. She felt like stopping to explain the situation, but what was the point? People believed what they wanted to believe.

Who cared? That was one of the main rules of life.

And if they believed the wrong things? Well, Melissa could always get back at them later. With a *vengeance*.

She couldn't help taking a quick look around, though, trying to read the faces, read the minds behind the faces. Any notebook authors here, folks?

No immediate suspects jumped to mind, but Melissa saw that Allison was very tense today. She held a pencil tight in one fist, point raised. Like a weapon.

She was also sitting in Melissa's seat.

Mr. Elliot had ignored their entrance; he was scribbling some notes. Finally he glanced up. "Go ahead and grab a seat, guys." Mr. Elliot hardly ever bothered with tardy slips, but he did have a long memory and a special way of making you feel edgy, guilty about walking in late. At least that's how Melissa felt; a lot of the others never seemed to care much. Melissa figured if you were constantly late that helped prove that you weren't taking Intervention seriously, leaving you just one more step closer to that big kick to Bannerston.

Russ took his time as always, but Melissa sat down right away, noticing, as she did, that the desk Russ trashed the day before was neatly stacked up in the back corner of the room, ready for someone to fix or toss in a trash dumpster.

Interesting.

Since Allison was sitting in Melissa's usual seat, she had no choice and wound up at the far end of the circle, next to Russ.

Wonderful.

Tracy Callahan was giving Melissa an odd look, and she wondered for a second what the look meant. Contempt? Admiration?

Also interesting.

"How is everybody today?" asked Mr. Elliot, walking over to take his seat inside the circle.

There were a few mumbles, but mostly everybody gave an upbeat answer. After all, there was no percentage in being a grouse or a complainer. Another lesson from Intervention: If life seems to be nothing but problems, maybe *you* are the problem.

Melissa had been the problem of her life for too long. She was more than ready to move on.

Popping gum as always, Allison squeezed her pencil and tried to look bored. Right. Melissa had a theory about Allison; she figured that the bored, very blasé look was a practiced act. Nobody could be that superficial this early in life.

Besides, what about the slam books? They were the big giveaway. If Allison was really so burned out, why would she care what anybody else thought or did? Behind that front Allison was a little too mixed up in everyone else's business.

Which was probably a cover for something else entirely. Maybe Allison was insecure. Maybe the reason she pretended not to care about anybody was because she was frightened of *everybody*, worried about her place in it all, concerned about what everybody thought of her.

Maybe Allison was just plain scared.

Wouldn't that be great?

Yeah. But if Allison was so easily pinned down, that brought up the next question: was she the author of the notebook? And, if so, was it a rambling joke or the ravings of a girl ready to snap?

It could happen; one had to consider the possibility. After all, how many times did you read in the papers about somebody, some post office employee or fast-food clerk or somebody who just went off one day, cracked, and ambled in to work with a gun, shooting everybody in sight?

It even happened at a school years ago; Melissa remembered reading about it. Some girl shot up a playground with her dad's hunting rifle. When she got busted and the cops asked her why she did it, the girl just shrugged the whole thing off and said, "I don't like Fridays."

Melissa stared over at Allison, quietly wondering. It's not Friday, it's Monday morning, girl. How you feeling?

Russ laughed out loud. "Another day in the Cracker Jack box."

Ignoring this, Mr. Elliot leaned back, picking it up like a conversation. "So what's everybody up to?"

Melissa bit her lip, waiting. She didn't look around, though. That would have been slightly uncool.

Russ said, "Well, I bagged the big Mo. Does that count?"

Melissa felt herself go red, but Mr. Elliot asked, "What do you mean?"

"I mean Melissa, I really zapped her." Russ told his version of the grease gun story from Terry the Terror's. Melissa didn't add anything, but Tracy shook her head, saying, "I suppose that makes you real proud, huh?"

"A little proud, yeah."

"You've got a long way to go."

"Yeah, like you don't."

"Enough," said Mr. Elliot, cutting them off.

Boris growled. "I almost clobbered my old man last night. Does that count?"

Smiling, Mr. Elliot said, "I guess that would depend on why you wanted to clobber him. But no, on second thought I don't think it does count, because you say you *almost* clobbered him. You didn't actually do it. Perhaps that means something good."

"Yeah," chuckled Tiny. "Or maybe he just wimped out."

"I didn't wimp out."

"Who was your old man smacking around this time?" This was from Russ, again trying to stir up trouble.

"Eh!" Boris barked this time. "If my old man smacks somebody, they probably almost deserved it."

" 'Probably almost?' "

"You heard me."

"Heard, yes. Understood, hardly."

"You're the one to talk."

Russ sat up. "Hey, I don't have to talk about things.

52

When my old man gets out of line with somebody in my family I step in. If I gotta take blows, I take blows."

"Why don't you just leave?" Melissa heard herself asking the question before she even realized she was doing it.

"Leave? And go where?"

"Anywhere. Somewhere."

"I gotta look after my sisters."

Mr. Elliot offered his typical suggestion. "There are agencies that can help . . ."

"No." Russ snapped back his answer and reminded Mr. Elliot of his day-one promise. "None of this goes out of this room, you don't call social workers or whatever."

Holding up his hand, Mr. Elliot agreed, probably for his own benefit as much as anyone's. "I don't make phone calls. I just think it might be a good idea if *you* made the call. Think about your sisters."

"I take care of them." Russ shrugged. "Besides, the old man ain't so bad. At least he stays around and pays the bills."

Good point, thought Melissa. She was thinking about her mother, but immediately diverted herself from that subject. Nothing good could possibly come of that. Mom was gone, a memory, she walked and she never looked back. So be it. It was her idea and she wasn't coming back.

Tracy spoke up, her eyes kind of starry. "You know, this reminds me of that new Walrus song, 'Light Years Above.' You guys hear it?"

Nobody had.

Tracy wasn't surprised. "My brother works at Tower Records, and we get all the stuff even before it's supposed to be released."

Gary Walden muttered, his first mutter of the morning. "There is no point to all of this," he said.

"Well, that's great to know."

"The point to all of this is understanding," said Mr. Elliot. He leaned forward to stress his point. "If we can establish some understanding here, some understanding between us, in this small group, then perhaps you'll take some of that understanding out into the world with you."

Allison had a very blank look on her face. "Why would anybody want to?"

Mr. Elliot shrugged. "That's up to you to decide."

Allison frowned.

None of the others did, though. They knew better; at least Melissa did. It was one thing to find yourself suddenly in Intervention, it was another thing to work yourself out.

Sometimes driver's ed seemed a long way away.

Melissa looked around, the question coming to her again. Any notebook authors there?

Hard to say. But there were plenty of suspects.

Things drifted along, as they did sometimes, and finally Mr. Elliot nodded toward the wall clock, as if it had just shouted a time warning to him. Hurrying up a bit, he got up for a second and went over to his desk, returning with a wooden box about two feet by one foot in size. Melissa knew what it was, they all did. Mr. Elliot said, "Let's take a couple of minutes to look through the Somebody box."

Groans. But they were a different sort of groan, groans of anticipation, because everybody was always curious about the Somebody box.

Mr. Elliot explained it as he always did, as a reminder. "The Somebody box is sort of a complaint/suggestion box, where you can put in things you want to say in class, but didn't work up to. No names required, just sort of a neat way to gauge how everyone is feeling about each other—and about himself. We needn't know *who* wrote the comment, because we know that *somebody* did.''

He always had to get that last part in, thought Melissa. That was the big Intervention thing: like yourself. Like yourself, like yourself, like yourself. A simple chant which, if you repeated it often enough, supposedly came true. Melissa had her doubts.

What Mr. Elliot didn't say, but what Melissa was pretty sure about, was that some of the comments stuffed in and pulled from the Somebody box were penned by none other than Mr. Elliot himself. Little fortune-cookie lessons for everyone. Read into that whatever you wanted.

The first Somebody comment pulled from the box amounted to very little. It was, ''When are we going to catch a break?''

Mr. Elliot laughed, looking up and around. ''Never,'' he laughed. ''Never a break for you guys.''

A lot of people laughed back, Melissa included.

The next Somebody question was more difficult. ''When are we actually going to see somebody get out of Intervention? When will anybody get to go back to their real life?''

Mr. Elliot nodded, thought just a moment and then answered. He said, ''This is a new program, we're sort of working it out as we go. Let's try to be patient.''

He smiled. As if that smile said it all.

On to the next.

Mr. Elliot frowned, because the next item was a white piece of cloth, with a piece of paper pinned to it. Mr. Elliot unpinned the paper from the cloth and read in a flat voice, letting the words slip out before he realized he shouldn't have. The last question, pinned, Melissa knew, to a torn chunk of lace sweater, was, ''Who do I have to kill to get my notebook back?''

Chapter 7

Who do I have to kill? Melissa jumped and she saw Mr. Elliot's eyes racing, moving from student to student, trying to figure out who wrote the note.

Melissa looked herself. Who? *Who?*

Anybody. It could be anybody.

Mr. Elliot was looking, waiting, but finally he gave up. "What's this? What is this nonsense?" Crunching the paper, he shook his head. "This isn't productive," he said. "This is not constructive . . ."

"What?" This was from Tracy, nervous as always. "What isn't constructive? What are you talking about?"

"Never mind." Mr. Elliot's eyes were cold.

Melissa blinked. Swallowed. Tried not to let her face betray her emotions. The torn bit of sweater was hers, there was going to be hell to pay for *that,* but most of all it was scary. Tearing up the sweater was a message someone was sending to her. So was the note. This was a situation, or at least it was becoming one, and she was going to need help. She had to talk to Holly, and she had to do it right away.

At the bell, though, Mr. Elliot spoke up, saying, "Melissa, could you hold back a minute?"

Oops.

The class emptied fast, it always did, but Melissa

was caught behind. Nailed. At first she thought maybe it was tardy slip time, but then she realized that couldn't be it. He practically never gave out tardy slips and besides, if he was suddenly giving out tardy slips he would have nailed Russ too. So she figured it had to be about the notebook, or the files Russ lifted, and she wasn't sure of what she might say if questioned.

Mr. Elliot waited until Tiny got out the door—he was the last to leave—and then he nodded to her. "You came in late with Russ."

"Yeah." Maybe it *was* a tardy slip. "I'm sorry, I got all caught up. I don't know what he was up to. I mean, we weren't together *together.*"

Mr. Elliot lifted a pencil, his expression blank. "Still, what do you think?"

"What do I think?" What did he mean?

"About Russ. You were sitting with him in the library Friday."

"Yeah, but he just came over and plopped down. I didn't ask him or anything."

"I know. Relax, Melissa, you don't have to defend yourself to me. I'm just curious. Worried about him, actually. I'm worried about Russ. He's a hard case."

Melissa rolled her eyes. "Yeah, tell me about it."

"Well, I was sort of hoping you'd tell me."

A little nervous, Melissa said, "I don't know what to tell."

Mr. Elliot held up the torn bit of sweater. "What about this? Do you think he might know anything about this?"

"I don't know."

"How about you? Know anything about this?"

"I . . ." For a second Melissa almost talked, almost told him all about it. Maybe Mr. Elliot could be the ally she needed.

No. On second thought she realized that Mr. Elliot

was the last person in the world she should tell. Her reputation was bad enough, no sense adding any more implications of instability and goofiness to whatever it was these people thought of her. If they—the school, the Powers—wanted to shove her square peg into a round hole, there was no sense in her greasing the thing up for them, was there?

"No," she said, "I don't know anything about it."

Mr. Elliot nodded. He picked up the torn bit of sweater and played with it for a few seconds. Then he said, "This looks expensive. Isn't it? I've seen you wearing it, remember. Last week."

Melissa cringed. That was right, she had worn it, to class, all over. Sheesh, that was the whole point of smuggling it out of the house, *of course* she wore it. And of course he recognized it. What was she supposed to say now?

"It's my stepmother's," she said. "I borrowed it, and I forgot to ask her, and . . ." Her voice trailed off.

Another nod from Mr. Elliot. "So what about it? Is Russ the type to rip up an expensive sweater?"

"How should I know?"

"He did break up that desk."

Melissa didn't say anything.

"He said he sprayed oil on another outfit of yours."

"That was different."

Mr. Elliot nodded once more. He was quiet a moment, leaving Melissa shifting her books about, uncomfortable. Finally Mr. Elliot asked, "Is Russ obsessing about you?"

"*What?*" The idea almost made her laugh. Obsessing? About her? "I don't even know what that means."

"Just what it sounds like. Does he always try to talk to you? Leave you notes? Follow you home?"

Mr. Elliot hesitated, as if he really didn't want to ask the next, but he did.

"Do you think he's spending an unhealthy amount of time thinking about you?"

Unhealthy? That was funny, but Melissa shook her head. "I think not."

"You think not." Mr. Elliot turned the phrase over, considering it, then leaned back in his chair and said, "If he was obsessing about me, I think I'd be worried about it."

Melissa swallowed. "You would, huh?"

"Absolutely. Obsession is a dangerous thing. It leads to dangerous activity. Sometimes things just get out of control . . ."

Melissa waited, but Mr. Elliot didn't go any further. Instead he asked another bunch of questions. "What does he do? What does he talk about? Anything odd?"

Melissa shrugged. "Depends on what you mean by odd?"

"There's something you should know. That's not the first threat I've pulled out of the Somebody box. The handwriting was forced, faked, but I've got a thought that maybe it's Russ's."

Melissa made a joke. "I didn't know Russ could write."

"He's focused on you. Pays you a lot of attention. Maybe too much attention. I notice these things."

Melissa smirked. "I don't think Russ pays much attention to anything besides Russ."

Mr. Elliot didn't reply to this. He just finished packing up to leave, taking a moment's pause, as if he was considering what was said. He was ready to walk out the door, but he stopped long enough to touch Melissa's arm; the sudden reach startled her, and she almost dropped her books. Mr. Elliot sighed and said, "That's one of the problems with control."

"What?"

"Control. Control's great when you have it, one big roller coaster ride to hell when you lose it."

Mr. Elliot pulled his books and files close to his chest, and turned away, leaving the classroom.

Melissa followed him out. The warning bell was ringing, she was going to be late to algebra again, big deal, but she was wondering about Mr. Elliot's last words. What were they supposed to mean?

What was she supposed to do?

One thing was for sure, for whatever it was worth she wasn't about to start ratting out Russ, even if it did turn out he was the guy who broke into her locker and trashed her stuff, the sweater included. If the school wanted to ship somebody out to Bannerston, they sure didn't need any excuses, and she sure wasn't about to make herself part of the evidence against him.

When things got weird, the weird had to stick together.

Walking the hall, Melissa looked back over her shoulder, watching, waiting. Mr. Elliot was gone, off to the teacher's lounge, so she wasn't watching him. She wasn't watching anything, really. What could she be waiting for? She had no idea. Why was she messing around? She needed to get to class.

Holly still wasn't around, but she probably just missed her since she wasted so much time lingering after Intervention. Unless she really was gone somewhere. Did Holly decide to ditch without her? Where did she go? To the donut place? Somewhere with somebody else? Home?

Melissa had no idea.

She needed to stop messing around. She needed to get to class before she wound up spending the rest of her life in detention. The last bell was ringing, and she was definitely running out of excuses.

Mrs. Hegg was definitely unimpressed. Melissa didn't even have to wait, she was given a tardy slip as soon as she walked in the door. *Wonderful.* Melissa collapsed into her seat, digging through her books, but—

Oh, no.

A note. There was a folded note stuffed into her algebra book, as long as a letter. Before she even opened it she knew where it came from and who wrote it. Whoever trashed her locker, the slime left her a note. She thought about all the things Mr. Elliot said about Russ, about how he thought Russ was obsessing about her. Was Russ the one? *It can't be . . .*

Ignoring Mrs. Hegg's blackboard scrawls, Melissa unfolded the paper. The writing was in blue fine-line marker pen, and Melissa felt a chill of fear rush up her spine as she read it, not breathing.

The note began, THERE COMES A TIME IN EVERY RELATIONSHIP WHEN THE REAL MYSTERY BECOMES FEAR—WHO FEARS WHO THE MOST. ME, YOU. CONSIDER THIS: EVEN THE MOST LOVING RELATIONSHIP IS BASED ON DESPERATE FEAR—FEAR OF LOSS, PERHAPS, OR FEAR OF DEATH . . .

Oh my God . . . Melissa almost choked, but then she realized this was a threat, a reference to the craziness in the notebook, the notebook she hadn't even really read, except for that one small part. Holly was the one who did all the reading; Melissa hadn't even gotten a chance to mull it over with her. What was this supposed to mean?

"Miss Maynard."

Melissa jumped; Mrs. Hegg had a piece of chalk aimed right at her head, a tiny white bullet.

"Do you have an answer for the question on the board?"

61

Question? Melissa wanted to laugh. She was oblivious to all of this, everything racing around in her head. Mrs. Hegg was asking a question, as if anybody cared. Squeezing her eyes closed a minute, Melissa tried to think clearly, but thinking clearly wasn't easy.

"Melissa."

"No, no, I don't know."

The class was quiet—no Intervention-type crowd here—but Mrs. Hegg frowned and said, "I might ask to see what it is you're reading."

"No." Melissa barked that out quick, because she knew Mrs. Hegg wasn't allowed to snatch anything out of her hands. The teacher could, of course, choose to just throw her out of class. She looked as if she was considering it, but instead she said, "Put your personal things away."

Melissa did. She wanted to toss it far away, but she knew she'd better not. Not yet. Not until she figured it out, what was going on, and how hard was that going to be? What kind of nonsense was this? She folded up the letter and tucked it back inside the book.

Mrs. Hegg wasn't finished with her. "I'll give you another chance to work out the question on the board."

It was taking everything she had just to keep her cool, so Melissa looked up and said, "I can't right now."

"Not right now?"

"No. I can't think. Sorry."

"That will reflect as a zero."

"Fine." A lot of her life was reflected as a zero, another bad grade wasn't going to change that. There were more important things to consider. She had her book under her palm, she could almost feel the note, stuffed a few pages down. It was like heat was rising from it. Ugly words.

It was Russ, of course. Melissa felt like growling his name, but that wasn't going to change anything. Mr. Elliot warned her, told her about him, was this it? What did he call it? *Obsessing?* Was this proof? She knew he was crazy, but was Russ somebody she needed to be afraid of?

Not likely. Now she was getting mad. She'd clean his clock for him, and if she couldn't do it herself, she'd get somebody else to do it for her. Curt maybe. Melissa had friends, or at least potential friends, and one person she sure wasn't scared of was Russell Morse.

What was it Holly said before? Oh, yeah; Melissa remembered now. You needed to know Rumpelstiltskin's name. If you could name him, if you knew who he was, then you could destroy him.

Holly knew Rumpelstiltskin's name. Big deal. Melissa wasn't at all impressed.

She needed some backup on this. In fact, Melissa spent so much time at lunch trying to find Holly that she never got around to eating. Big deal, she could always afford to lose some pounds, but where was Holly?

Who knew? She did see Russ, though, standing—his back against the wall—in the middle yard, inside the chain-link fence, goofing off with a couple of his hairball friends. He looked up, gave Melissa the eye, and that did it. That broke it.

With nothing better to do, Melissa walked over and slapped him across the face.

Chapter 8

"Ow!" Russ looked totally surprised, but his friends broke into a half-cheer, clapping hands. They were real juveniles, not stuck in Intervention yet, but they probably belonged there. "Ho, ho, here we go," one of them said. "Go for it, babe, rock him."

Melissa turned on the guy. He was grinning and his teeth were yellow. She felt like hitting him too.

"What are you doing?" Russ's brain had caught up with the red smack mark on his face and he was ticked off now. Melissa couldn't think of anything immediately brilliant to say, so she hauled back to slap him again.

"No way," said Russ, grabbing her arm. "You slap me again and I'll bite you."

Russ's three goony friends loved this too, laughing again. Russ moved away from them, though, dragging Melissa by the arm. "What's wrong with you? I'll pay for your blouse, okay? Sheesh."

"I just want you to leave me alone."

"I thought I *was* leaving you alone."

"Just stop messing with me."

Russ shrugged. "All right, I'll stop. Just don't go ballistic. I liked messing with you."

"It's not at all funny."

"Sorry."

64

"You're lucky I didn't report you."

"Report me? You told Mr. Elliot and the whole world of psychobabble."

"I mean the note. *You're sick.* I should give it to Mr. Ramirez. Or Mr. Elliot. He's looking for you now, I think. Mr. Elliot thinks you might be dangerous. I'll say."

Russ frowned. "What note? What are you screeching about?"

"I'm not scared of you. I know who you are."

"Yeah? Who am I?"

"Just another creep."

"That's me," agreed Russ. "I'm one of the creeps."

"Besides, I didn't even read your stupid notebook. Holly's got it. If you want it back so bad, go ask her."

"What notebook?"

"Like you don't know. And I didn't appreciate you trashing my locker."

Shaking his head, Russ said, "You're a little loony, aren't you?"

"Loony? I'll show you loony, I—"

"Hey." Russ got her attention. "One, I didn't write you any note. Two, I'm not missing any notebooks, and three, I sure didn't trash your locker. Why would I?"

"Just stay out of my stuff."

"I said why would I? Now why would I?"

"You know why."

"I don't know. And if you try to slap me again I'll tie your hands behind your back and make you carry your books in your teeth." Taking a breath, Russ backed off some himself. "I said I'll pay you back for the blouse. I'm going to work for this garage, cleaning parts for this guy . . . ."

"I don't have time to listen to your life story."

Russ looked offended, maybe a little hurt. "Sorry."

He *did* look sorry. Now Melissa was confused, and she was looking around, hoping Holly would come along and rescue her. No such luck. All of a sudden she felt out of place and foolish. Russ seemed to catch the change because he walked with her, ignoring his friends. Russ said, "You want to tell me what else is going on in your life?"

"No."

He nodded. First he looked around, then he said, "Okay, you want to tell me why all of a sudden you're a maniac?"

That made her laugh; almost, anyway. "Not hardly."

"So what's this notebook thing you're talking about?"

Melissa almost told him, but then she thought better of it and shook her head. "Nothing. No big deal."

"No big deal." Another nod. "You find somebody's diary or something?"

"Or something." Leaning back against the chain-link fence, she took a deep breath.

"So what does that mean?"

"I told you, go ask Holly."

All of a sudden Russ looked a little sheepish. "She's your friend, I don't even know her."

"Your loss."

"Sheesh, you're strange today," said Russ. The first afternoon bell was ringing, so he turned on his heels and rejoined his buddies. Melissa shrugged. What was she supposed to say? Come to think of it, why was she even talking to Russ? Just because he put on a good front didn't mean he wasn't guilty of anything. Maybe he was a complete nut, unable to even tell right from wrong.

Or maybe not.

Melissa's first afternoon class was World History, taught by Mr. Treih, a very loud and frizzy-red-haired teacher, a sort of carrot-topped Einstein with an attention-span problem who spent more hours telling college fraternity stories than actually going over the textbook. They were playing World History Jeopardy, a variation of the TV game show that had Mr. Treih kicked back behind his desk, wooden pointer in one hand, flipping through index cards for good questions.

The category was Civil War battles, and Mr. Treih had the pointer aimed at Mark Wallace, indicating he was next in his row to answer (the class was divided into three groups, competing against each other). Mr. Treih started off with the question, but there was a knock on the door, and Holly walked in.

Melissa almost jumped and yelled at her, but right away she realized Holly was just playing office runner again, bringing a pile of notes in to Mr. Treih. He took the stack and glanced quickly through, checking to see if anything demanded an immediate reply. When he was distracted Holly waved at Melissa, an "I need to see you" nod. She even pulled the notebook to the top of the bundle she was carrying to show she still had it.

Melissa groaned, frowning. This was news? She'd been trying to see Holly all day; what was going on? Melissa gave her a "Come on and give me a break" look.

Holly signaled back that obviously she couldn't talk now. Or at least that's what it looked like. It occurred to Melissa that her interpretation wasn't exactly chiseled in stone. For all she knew Holly was giving the nautical signal for raise sail and hoist anchor; who knew?

Mr. Treih looked up, a little confused. "Well, this

is all well and good but none of this means a thing to me.''

Holly laughed. ''Me either.''

''Seriously though, I think this is supposed to go to Elliot. Try it on the basement guy and see what he thinks.''

''Yes, sir,'' said Holly, glowing. Melissa felt like bouncing a wad of paper off her head. Get your mind straight, girl; that's what she was thinking. It wasn't hard to see that Mr. Treih was one of Holly's many crushes. She took back the small stack of notes and left, giving Melissa another quick sign as she did. See you later and wait for me. Either that, or maybe prepare to lower the lifeboats.

Both were probably appropriate.

Melissa got into the Jeopardy game, even answering a question, or questioning an answer, actually. ''Lincoln's vice president,'' said Mr. Treih.

Nobody answered so Melissa raised a hand; the pointer fell towards her. ''Who was Lyndon Johnson?''

''Eeeeh!'' Mr. Treih barked out a buzzer noise. ''Almost, halfway, give you five points for that since you answered in the form of a question. Real guy was Andrew Johnson. Lyndon was part of the other civil war, the one over Vietnam. You know, 'Hey, Hey, L.B.J.?' ''

Melissa shook her head, not knowing what he was talking about but figuring that Mr. Treih was about to launch into one of his twenty-minute stories. He was. Even the arrival of an ambulance outside the front of the building didn't slow him down; ambulances weren't that big a deal. The nurse was required to call one for almost every slight injury, an out-of-control nosebleed or somebody getting hurt in wood shop. One came by about once a week, so Mr. Treih continued with his tale. It took the bell to interrupt him, and when it did he was halfway through telling about his draft physical. The bell rang and nobody moved. "Out of here," he said, waving the pointer. "I'll finish up on Monday. Tell you how peanut butter can keep any honest dude out of the army."

Melissa filed out with the others, wandering down the hall and looking around for Holly. Looking for news, really. After all, she still had this twisted note to deal with, the one Russ claimed to know nothing about, although he sure acted funny. Of course there was something to be said about Russ always acting funny.

She pulled the note out again and started to read it while she walked down the hall. THERE COMES A TIME IN EVERY RELATIONSHIP WHEN THE REAL MYSTERY BECOMES FEAR—WHO FEARS WHO THE MOST . . .

She skipped on down to a creepy passage: MY SYMPATHY FOR YOU IS AS MY SYMPATHY FOR THE DEAD. FOR I AM BECOME DEATH, DESTROYER OF WORLDS. FOR YOU, THERE IS ONLY ME OR THE LOT. TO ME, ALREADY YOU BREATHE NO MORE . . .

"*Gotcha.*"

Melissa jumped, ready to punch. Russ had his arm around her waist and she pushed him away. He even laughed when she raised her arm as if to smack him. "Hey, come on, you ready to stop being weird?"

Melissa shook her head. "I'm always weird."

"You don't need to tell me twice."

Melissa walked, but she didn't exactly race to outrun him. "So where's your goony friends?"

Shrugging, Russ said, "Friends? Ah, I don't have many friends. Those are just the guys I hang with, you know?"

"No, I don't know." Melissa tucked away the note again. "Have you seen Holly?"

"Only in my daydreams."

"Funny." Melissa looked around, not laughing.

Following along, Russ asked, "You walking home again today?"

"Why? You want to attack me again?"

"Maybe I do."

"I carry mace in my purse, you know."

That impressed Russ. "Do you? Really?"

"Absolutely." It was true—an antirape weapon from the ever psychotic Jeanette the Witch.

Russ laughed. "No thank you. Would you mace me for just wanting to walk home *with* you?"

" 'With you?' " That made Melissa laugh, but feel a little funny at the same time. Funny strange, as if part of her was considering it. Or maybe even wanting it. "Why would I want to walk *anywhere* with you, much less to my house?"

"Come on," he said, putting on his most winning voice, looking just a little less psycho. Question: what was he doing up here in the first place? Camping out and waiting just for her? That was enough to give a person the willies. Mr. Elliot said he was obsessing after all . . .

Obsessing or not, Russ was talking. He said, "I don't have to walk all the way to your house. Part of the way would be cool."

"I walk home with Holly. No, thanks."

"I could go with both of you."

"Oh, yeah, I'm sure she'd love that."

Russ didn't answer. She needed to go downstairs for her next class, so she walked on ahead but something was going on, something was blocking the top of the down staircase. Kids were all bunched up but nobody was moving, they were all gawking at something.

"What's this?" asked Russ.

"How should I know?" She didn't have any time for this, but Melissa was as curious as anybody. There was a boy with a set of stereo headphones pulled down around his neck. Russ grabbed him and asked, "What's going on, man?"

"Some girl fell over the rail, down the steps."

"What?" Melissa pushed forward.

The boy nodded. "Yeah, I guess she took a dive. Pitched right over and kissed the bottom of the stairs."

"Oh my God."

"Yeah, it's spooky."

Spooky. Melissa felt a chill, and she found herself pushing through the crowd. No, *please.* She pushed forward, down the steps, and she saw first the back of a white paramedic's jacket; two guys were lifting an unconscious girl who lay flat on her back on an ambulance gurney.

It was Holly.

I read somewhere once that all true stories are romances that end in death. I suppose my babble falls into this category; there's certainly plenty of death. All that's missing is the romance.

The day I found out about Mister Vanzetti started just like every other day in my life at that time. Slow and terrible and empty.

The first in my neighborhood to wake up each morning, I was the last who needed to bother. The last real worker, the last with obligations to rise and face each day, the last who trekked back each evening, wondering whether the burden was worth shouldering.

Mornings were difficult for me, because each act of waking was a slap of realization, a frightening moment when I had to confront not only the world, but myself, every day of my life. Later, during most of the day, I would be too busy or distracted to deal with it, but mornings were quiet. Just me and the terrifying reflection in the bathroom mirror . . .

Chapter 9

Oh my God . . .

Her heart fluttering, Melissa nearly collapsed, falling down herself, but she managed to recover, looking around desperately. What? *How?* How did it happen? This was crazy, how could Holly fall over the railing?

They were taking Holly outside.

"Wait, wait, *please.*"

One of the paramedics held up a hand. He had a bushy brown mustache and a tanned face that showed absolutely no emotion whatsoever. "Stand back, back off."

Melissa tried to follow them anyway, but someone grabbed her shoulders, pulling her back. It was Mr. Elliot. He said, "Melissa, hold on, come back out of the way."

She allowed him to pull her back, but at the same time felt herself breaking down, tears streaming down her cheeks. "Please . . ."

"Melissa, she'll be all right."

"Did you find her?"

He shook his head. "No. Mrs. Adison found her. I guess she fell from the third-floor railing."

No! Melissa refused to accept that. "She didn't fall."

"She did."

"No!" Pulling herself away from his grasp, Melissa dropped to her knees, scrambling around to pick up Holly's scattered books; Holly would need them later. Her English book was sprawled open over by a radiator; Melissa crawled over to grab it. If you lost your books you might have to pay for them later. She'd keep them; yes, she could do that. Melissa figured she would just stash them in her locker until later, until . . .

Oh my God.

She got up now and pushed through the big doors, following after the ambulance crew, running across the lawn after them. The white and blue truck was parked in the front fire lane, its overhead lights flashing. "Wait. Please." They were lifting Holly into the back of the ambulance; the guy with the mustache slammed the door shut and moved to climb in up front. Melissa grabbed onto his sleeve, pleading, saying, "Wait, where's she going? She's my best friend. Which hospital?"

"U.M.C.," the guy answered automatically.

University Medical Center. Melissa knew where that was. "Can I come."

"Not with us, sorry."

The driver climbed in, the ambulance pulled away, and Melissa looked around, a little desperate, trying to figure out what to do. She needed to follow Holly to the hospital, needed to get there to be with her now, but how?

Kids were crowding outside, but it wasn't just kids, there were a few teachers outside too. Everybody was confused, worrying. Mr. Elliot was outside now, and he came up beside her and touched Melissa on the shoulder. "What can I do?"

Tears were still running down Melissa's cheeks. She

didn't know how to express herself. "I need to go with her. I need to get to the hospital."

He didn't hesitate. "Okay. I'll drive you. Come on."

"Come on?"

"Yes, come on with me."

He led her to the teacher's lot. Mr. Elliot's car looked new, but probably it wasn't. A shiny Chevy of some kind. One thing Melissa noticed was a funky smell, anyway. A sort of musky dampness. He suggested she roll down the window. "I think I ran down a cat or something."

"A cat?" Melissa sniffed, pulling herself together. Every moment felt a little more oppressive, so she did roll down the window.

"Nothing good, anyway." Mr. Elliot shrugged, then said, "Listen, it'll probably be too late today, but I'll get you a pass. Keep Ramirez from jumping all over you about leaving."

Melissa appreciated that, and she said, "Thanks."

"No problem."

Choking back a sigh, Melissa asked, "What about you?"

"What?" He didn't seem to understand the question.

Melissa looked up from her fingers; she was chewing on them. Nerves. "How can you just take off from school?"

Mr. Elliot forced a smile. "Don't worry about me. I'm pretty much wrapped up for the day. Let's worry about Holly."

"I am."

He nodded. "I am too."

They got to U.M.C. quickly; Melissa was sure the ambulance couldn't have beaten them by more than a few minutes. After he parked the car, Mr. Elliot led her toward the emergency entrance, bypassing the waiting seats and aiming straight for the reception nurse, a big blonde lady perched behind a counter. Melissa started rattling at the lady, speaking fast, saying, "You just brought a girl in, she got hurt in a fall and the ambulance brought her, and her name's Holly Edinger and I need to know if she's all right and—"

"Take a breath."

"What?"

The nurse spoke, slow and calm. "Take it easy, just take it easy."

"I need to see Holly."

"Well, she's in treatment room one right now," said the nurse. "Are you family?"

"A teacher from school." Mr. Elliot sat his palms on the counter, waiting.

The nurse looked at Melissa. "I'm her best friend," she answered. "I need to be with her."

The nurse was all sympathy, but she said, "That won't really work right now."

"What happened?"

"That's impossible to say."

Melissa felt desperate. "Is she going to be all right?"

"I'm sure she will."

"What sort of an answer is that?"

"It's the best I can give you right now."

"Oh my God."

"Please, we're very busy. You need to relax."

"Marcy."

The voice was that of a doctor, walking from one of the treatment rooms and toward the counter. The big nurse acknowledged her name and the doctor kept talking, saying, "Once we've got this girl stabilized we'll move her to ICU three, I think. Have we gotten hold of her parents?"

"We're working on that, doctor."

ICU. Melissa knew what that meant: intensive care unit. However Holly was, it wasn't so good.

Melissa grabbed the medic by the sleeve of his white lab coat. "I need to see her."

He shook his head even as he pushed a stethoscope into his pocket. "She's not even conscious. She . . ."

Ignoring that, Melissa dropped his sleeve and rushed past him, into the sparse treatment room. The doctor and the nurse called after her, but neither chased after her inside. She walked around the curtain and saw. Flat on a table, no pillow under her head, Holly looked terrible, almost gray in color. She had a clear IV tube in her right arm, a dark blue one snaking from somewhere up her nose.

The left side of her face was swollen, red and blue.

Her eyes were closed. Worse than that, they looked as if they had never, ever been open.

Melissa shuddered. Holly's left hand wasn't wired into anything terrifying, so Melissa squeezed that, fighting her own tears. Her heart jumped in surprise, though, when she saw Holly's eyelids flutter, as if there were some great effort in raising them. She seemed to be gasping for air to speak, and Melissa bent down to hear.

"Yahhh . . ."

"What?" *Oh my God*, thought Melissa, she can't breathe, she can't breathe. "Hey!" Melissa looked around, yelling for help. "Somebody! Somebody help!"

"Pleeese."

"I'm here."

"Hahh . . . help me . . ."

"I will. *Somebody! Please!*" Melissa yelled out again.

"Yahhhs . . . Yales. . . ."

"Yales?" She strained to hear what Holly was trying to say.

77

"Yaees lot. *Yales* lot. Lot, lot, lot . . ."

Holly's eyes flickered shut. She was passing out, just as the doctor and his nurse and Mr. Elliot all rushed into the treatment room. "Step back," said the doctor. "Stand back, what's happening?"

"She woke up. She talked."

Mr. Elliot's eyebrows shot up. "She did?"

Melissa nodded. "Yes, she wanted help."

"Help?" The doctor asked this as he bent over, raising one of Holly's eyelids.

"That's what she said."

"Well . . . that's what we're here for."

The nurse nodded. "We'll help her."

"Come on," said Mr. Elliot, taking Melissa by the shoulders. "Let's back out, let's get out of the way."

She let him lead her out into the corridor. That was where he asked, "Are you going to be all right?"

Melissa shook her head. "No. But I'll hang on."

Mr. Elliot nodded. "Okay."

They sat down and waited together. Holly's mom and dad got there a few minutes later, but neither noticed Melissa, or at least they didn't pay much attention to her. She started to feel a little awkward, as if she really was somehow in the way. Mr. Elliot offered to drive her home, and finally she nodded in answer. She needed to get out of there.

Melissa gave him directions when they got into his car. His eyebrows went up again. "You walk to school through the Vanzetti? I didn't know many people did that."

"Sometimes. It's not so bad in the daytime. We just cut through, anyway."

He nodded, started the car. "We're just about through with daytime. We better get you home."

Mr. Elliot drove. As he did he adjusted his hands on the steering wheel and started talking. "You said Holly woke up for a while? Asked for help?"

"Yeah."

"Is that all she said?"

Melissa shrugged. "That and some weird stuff."

"Weird stuff?"

She had been thinking, and Melissa changed the subject to ask about Russ. "Do you really think he's obsessing about me?"

"I think it might be possible. I'm hardly a psychiatrist; I'm not one to make judgments."

"Does he scare you?"

"What?"

She swallowed and asked again. "Does Russ ever scare you?"

Mr. Elliot considered that a minute. "Yes. Sometimes I think Russ does scare me."

Melissa nibbled on her lip. She was hoping he would say no, Russ never scared him. Russ wasn't a scary kind of guy. Because he didn't, Melissa had to ask the next question. "Do you think Russ could do something like that? Push Holly over that railing?"

Mr. Elliot's eyes narrowed a lot now. "What exactly did Holly say to you, Melissa?"

"Nothing like that. Nothing about how she got hurt, but she was scared and I got this note before, I think it was from Russ, but he . . ." She didn't finish. She let herself be distracted, and it wasn't hard to find a reason. This was strange, the way Mr. Elliot was taking to drive her home, this route. The sun was down now, and this was a place of dark, hollow-looking houses. Empty-looking places, corners with lonely-looking stop signs and no streetlamps. Melissa didn't recognize the neighborhood, and she said so. "Where are we?"

Mr. Elliot kept his eyes on the dark road now. "This is a shortcut. I know where we're going."

"Seems out of the way."

"It is, a little. What else did Holly say?"

"Something weird which didn't make sense."

"Maybe it will to me."

"She said 'Yale's Lot.' "

Mr. Elliot looked over at her. "Yail's Lot? Y-A-I-L? Yail?"

"I guess. I thought it was Y-A-L-E."

"No."

"You know what she was talking about?"

He nodded, considering it. "Yeah. It's something Russ was talking about, a long time ago."

"Russ?" Melissa felt sick again.

Mr. Elliot saw her go pale and he shook his head right away. "Hey, this doesn't mean Russ had anything to do with anything. You understand that?"

"Yes, but . . . we should tell somebody."

"I don't think we should. Not until we know something for sure."

"But what if he did it?"

"What if he didn't?" Mr. Elliot's stare was intense. "You know the sort of pressure an Intervention student is under; you're under that very same microscope yourself. Maybe I'm going too far to watch out for him, but I'm willing to do that—I'd do it for you."

"I don't care about Russ, I'm worried about Holly."

"But what if he didn't do anything? You know how it works with Intervention students. Ramirez would ship Russ out for Bannerston on general principles, just for his name coming up in an investigation, whether he did anything wrong or not."

Confused for a second, Melissa said, "Yeah, I know, but . . ."

"Think how you'd feel."

She shook her head. "This isn't about all that stuff. Holly's in the hospital."

"Yes, and you don't have any reason to think Russ is involved."

"You said yourself this Yail's Lot stuff came from him."

"Not from *him*." Mr. Elliot caught himself, took a breath. "Listen," he said. "I need you to promise me you won't mention anything about Russ to anyone."

Melissa wasn't about to promise anything. Why was Mr. Elliot all of a sudden trying to protect Russ? Why would anyone protect Russ if he did this? Melissa said, "I need to get home."

"I'll get you there. I think I need to show you something first."

"Show me?"

"Yes."

"I didn't even call. I don't think anybody even knows where I am."

"I realize that."

Melissa suddenly realized that herself.

Mr. Elliot slowed the car to a crawl. "There," he said. "Off to the right."

She looked. There was an old, dead-looking Victorian house with a spiked iron fence around it, but more importantly there was a cluttered field beside it, off to the left, its grounds overgrown with weeds and junk. "That's why they call this chunk of town the Vanzetti," said Mr. Elliot.

"Yeah?"

"Yeah. There used to be a house there on that lot. The old man—Yail Vanzetti—he owned all of that, the house, the lot. Now there's just a junk pile, a big rusting dinosaur. Old car parts, sinks, tools, splintered wood, broken windows, jagged edges. Razor sharp edges—that pile has teeth, it bites."

"It bites?"

"Yeah." Mr. Elliot was lost in his own thoughts now. Why? What did all of this have to do with anything? "That's Yail's Lot," he said. "When I was a kid my sister used to walk me home and we had to go past it, that was right after the fire. My sister never missed a challenge.''

Melissa swallowed. She was thinking about Holly now, feeling terrible that she had forgotten, even for an instant. Holly never missed a challenge. Melissa just wanted to get home.

Mr. Elliot didn't start the car going again, though, not right away. He looked over at Melissa and the only light on his face now was that bounding off of the clouds and coming off of the car's dashboard. ''Yail's Lot,'' he said, shaking his head as if he just thought of something funny. ''Russ didn't make up Yail's Lot, Melissa. He just knows about it. He talks about it. He grew up around here, and so did I.''

She swallowed. ''You did?''

Mr. Elliot did laugh now. ''Yeah. That's where the bodies are buried . . .''

Chapter 10

"Bodies?" A little bit startled, Melissa swallowed, suddenly apprehensive, wondering if maybe she should be nervous. A little nervous.

Mr. Elliot smiled, embarrassed, seeming to back away. "Sorry. That body thing's nothing Russ actually said, just an old line I remember hearing all the time, when I was a kid. I don't think it means actual bodies, more like secrets. You know, hidden things. Burying the past." He grabbed the gearshift, pulling the car back into drive. Smiled. "Forget I said that. It's nothing important."

Isn't it? Really? Melissa thought a long moment, staring long and hard at Mr. Elliot as he drove. It occurred to her that so far today she had spent more time with the Intervention instructor than she ever had before, and heard some things maybe she would have been better off not hearing, not knowing, which was odd, since it was all supposed to make her feel better. As for the circumstances, well, it probably didn't matter. Time in Intervention was never supposed to be pleasant.

Shifting in her seat, Melissa turned and watched the neighborhood grow a little better as they got closer to her house—or was this just a prejudice? It was all more than a little strange, if you asked her. All of a sudden she had the crazy thought of wanting out of the car, away from Mr. Elliot, but what was she supposed to do? Jump from a moving vehicle?

Besides, he was definitely taking her home now. They were out of the Vanzetti and it wasn't really that much farther, considering. They turned onto a street she recognized and Mr. Elliot broke his silence, saying, "We're just about there now, eh?"

"Yeah." Melissa nodded, turning her attention back to the road, still lost in thought. She felt as if things were swirling around her, as if she was stuck in some wind tunnel while items from her life blew about, out of control. First thing she was going to do when she got home was call the hospital, check on Holly. Get some control back.

"Come see me tomorrow."

"What?" She just looked at him.

"Before homeroom, I mean." Keeping his eyes on the road, Mr. Elliot explained. "I'll get you a pass for the office."

Melissa nodded, but she didn't say anything, not right away. It was occurring to her that Mr. Elliot might have his own agenda working here. He was trying to protect Russ, that much was clear already. Why? And how far would he go to do it?

Could Russ really have pushed Holly over that railing? What was she trying to say when she said Yail's Lot?

They were there now, outside Melissa's house. Mr. Elliot didn't pull into the driveway, but rather slid the car up alongside the curb. The lights were bright inside, so Jeanette the Witch was definitely at home; Melissa wouldn't need her keys. Wonderful . . .

Mr. Elliot caught on to her distress and raised an eyebrow. "Do you want me to come to the door with you?"

Shaking her head, Melissa said, "No. Thanks, anyway. I'll be all right."

"It's no trouble."

"Yeah, I think it would be. Jeanette's in there and she'd drag you into a long conversation." Brushing some hair from her eyes, Melissa said, "If there's one thing I couldn't stand right now it would be listening to that. I'd go from being a person to being a *topic*. I don't think I'm up to being a topic right now."

Mr. Elliot smiled, weak but sincere. "Yes, I understand that. Well, have a good evening."

"I doubt it."

"Try. Holly will be all right, I'm sure."

"I hope."

"Do what you can."

"I will." Melissa popped the door handle and got out.

The rush of the fresh air over her was shocking, as if being free of the musky car interior was like crawling out of some tomb; she gasped a deep breath before even realizing she was doing it. The breeze was cool and clean, smelling only slightly of distant burning leaves. The sort of pollution nobody really minded. She waited for Mr. Elliot to pull away, but he just sat there in his dark car, watching her.

Probably he just wanted to make sure she got inside all right. Fine, that was nice of him. She started up the walk to the house, thinking again about Holly, the things she said, and how nice Mr. Elliot was to be there, to drive her up to the hospital, to . . .

Melissa listened to the sounds. The leaves. Her footfalls. Jeanette's crazy dogs running around inside of the house. The vague, faint noises of the neighborhood that became almost a melody if you sat outside, or left your window open in the dark. Like a quiet animal breathing at your feet, or your own breathing, and a thundering heartbeat rising above it all . . .

Mr. Elliot was still there, parked, watching her.

Why? She had her hand on the door handle now, ready to twist it and go inside, but she wanted Mr. Elliot to leave. She was waiting for him to go, pull away, get out of here.

But he stayed. She could see him, no, untrue, she couldn't *see* him, just his shape, a sulking shadow inside his car, a shadow that wouldn't leave.

She had the door, she could open it, she could go inside and close it behind her, but no. He had to leave. It was important to Melissa that he leave, that the shadow drive away, that—

Snap! The doorknob pulled out of her hand, the door opened, and suddenly Jeanette the Witch was there in all her glory. *"Well?"* Her eyes darted back and forth like pinballs, Melissa thought. Justice aside, judgment had already been pronounced in her absence. Typical. Jeanette said, "You're in enough trouble, are you going to make it worse by standing out there all night?"

Melissa felt the strength slipping from her. No time to even come up with a story, aside from the truth. She followed Jeanette inside and steeled herself for it. When she turned to close the door behind her, she saw that the shadow—Mr. Elliot—was gone.

Creepy.

Jeanette gave her all of three feet of space, turning immediately to start the inquisition. "Let's have it, go ahead. I can't wait to hear this one."

"Holly's in the hospital."

"Is she?"

"I'm serious."

"I'm sure you are. Do you realize it's almost six o'clock?"

Frustrated, Melissa tossed her books over on the

86

couch. Another habit Jeanette the Witch hated, but too bad. "I just told you, Holly's in the hospital. I was with her. She's not even awake, she's hurt bad."

Jeanette didn't jump right on Melissa's challenge. Instead she nodded, a vague sort of nod, and asked, "How did this happen?"

"She fell from a third-floor stairwell. I don't know what happened exactly, but I think maybe I'm a part of it."

"A part of it? How's that? Did you push her?"

"No."

"Then how can you be a part of it?"

"I'm not real sure."

"I didn't figure you were."

"Hey, I'm trying to tell you what happened to me today. You're supposed to care."

Jeanette listened, but she wasn't much amused. She said, "It sounds to me like you just picked yourself another excuse to ditch school."

"I didn't ditch school."

"Right."

"My best friend was hurt. I care what happens to her."

"Spare me the lengthy explanations."

"You're supposed to listen to me, Jeanette, you're supposed to care what I have to say, you're—"

Ring!

The telephone was ringing, but Melissa ignored it, trying to keep Jeanette's attention. "I want to talk to you."

Ring!

Jeanette answered the phone, spoke, and then listened for a long while. Every once in a while she would toss in a short comment, but Melissa couldn't hear what she might be saying, and was hardly interested. Finally Jeanette hung up and turned. "Well, then."

Melissa bent over the couch and recovered her books. "Well, then, what?"

Jeanette smirked. "That was your special education teacher."

"I'm not in special education."

"Whatever it is, Mr. Elliot his name is—"

"Intervention." Melissa glared.

Jeanette nodded. "So that was your Intervention teacher."

"Wonderful."

"He called to back up your story."

"It's not a story."

"Whatever; he says what *you* say is true, and unlike you he's willing to talk about things."

"Right." Mr. Elliot, what was he up to? Was he this determined to protect Russ? Why? Especially since he acted so sure that Russ wasn't involved in the first place.

Jeanette was still talking. "So I think you should talk to your father in the morning."

Melissa nodded again, starting toward the stairs. "Right."

"I'm going to talk to him."

Melissa nodded. "I'm sure you will."

Melissa was sure. She wanted to talk to her father in the morning, get her side of the story out, but he was late getting home again and she couldn't wait. She walked to school, but wasted no time and made no diversions. Once she got there she cheated the bell and totally ignored going to homeroom or anything; she went straight to the office and talked to the secretary, a red-headed woman named Mrs. Hodges. Melissa placed her books on the counter and said, "I need to see the vice principal."

The secretary nodded; this wasn't exactly news to her. "Who sent you?"

"Nobody sent me this time, I'm here on my own."

"Missing homeroom? Without a pass?"

Melissa considered the stop at Mr. Elliot's office, which she had avoided. "I need to see Mr. Ramirez."

Mrs. Hodges frowned, unimpressed. "Grab a seat, I'll check with him."

Melissa waited. The secretary came out a moment later and said, "Go on in."

Melissa did. Vice Principal Ramirez was seated behind his desk, flipping through some files. He was a big man, with a charcoal-gray suit and a pencil-thin black mustache. All the girls Melissa knew figured Ramirez thought himself the hottest thing alive; most of the girls disagreed. "Grab a seat," he said, without even looking up. There was a cup of coffee on his desk and he took a sip.

Melissa settled herself. "I need to talk to you about Holly," she said.

Mr. Ramirez frowned. "The accident? What do you know about that?"

Swallowing, a little nervous now, Melissa said, "I don't know anything about it. But I got this note. It's about this notebook I found and Holly read."

"Notebook? What notebook?"

"I don't have it anymore."

"Yes?"

Melissa took a breath. A deep one. "I think somebody is out to get me."

"Out to get you?" Mr. Ramirez almost laughed; he did take another sip of coffee.

"Yeah."

"What's that got to do with Holly's accident?"

"I think this person got her first."

"What person is this?"

"I don't know. I'm not sure. I've got an idea, maybe . . ."

89

Mr. Ramirez looked unimpressed. "Why would anyone want to get you?"

"Like I said, it's about this notebook."

"This notebook you don't have anymore."

"Yeah."

Mr. Ramirez shook his head, it was obvious he wasn't taking all of this too seriously. "You're in my office a lot, Melissa."

"I know, but this is important. Somebody pushed Holly down those steps."

"That was an accident, Melissa."

"*No.* Look, there's something bad going on here."

"Bad?"

"Yeah, you know. Bad crazy, maybe. I told you, I got a note. A threat."

Ramirez frowned, leaning back in his seat, the joints of the chair squeaking. "Okay. Let me see the note."

Melissa nodded. She untucked the paper from her algebra book and handed it over.

Frowning, Ramirez read. He appeared to look it over several times, then opened up the file in front of him again and flipped through some papers.

Melissa waited, tense. She felt a little awkward, embarrassed about going behind Mr. Elliot's back, about not doing what he asked, giving him some time, but all of a sudden she felt a little creepy just thinking about him. Something weird was going on, and the Intervention instructor was maybe a part of it. Whether he really was trying to cover up for Russ, or whether it might be something worse she didn't know. She . . .

Let it go. She sat there waiting now, waiting for him to pick up the telephone and call the police, call the FBI, call *somebody*, do *something*.

That wasn't exactly how he reacted.

Leaning back in his chair, he shook his head and

said, "You understand why I'm not exactly jumping around the room?"

"No."

"Please, Melissa."

Feeling for a second like she was going crazy, Melissa said, "Aren't you going to do something about this?"

Vice Principal Ramirez shook his head, a long, slow gesture of what Melissa saw as growing contempt in his eyes. "Look at your file," he said, pushing it across the desk. "Go on, take a look."

Melissa made no move to open the file.

"There's a lot of nonsense in there. A lot of nonsense."

"I know, but—"

"Wait, I'm not finished." Mr. Ramirez sneered. "The file shows a long record of false alarms about things. You are definitely the girl who cried wolf."

"I know, and I'm sorry, but—"

"No, it doesn't work that way." Mr. Ramirez shook his head. "Holly's your friend, isn't she?"

"Yes."

"That's what I thought. That's why this really surprises me, I think." Mr. Ramirez sighed. "Come on, Melissa," he said, "Don't you think I know what's going on here? A joke. Your best friend is in the hospital and you're just a creepy enough girl to build a sick practical joke from it . . ."

Unlike our yard, the Vanzetti yard was always beautiful because Mr. Vanzetti was a meticulous man, still concerned with the upkeep of his house, lawn, and garden, especially after his wife died. His was always the last green of the year, the last grass to surrender to winter sleep. Hours he spent in his lot, the huge field beside his house, tending, nurturing his garden, and every fall he wound up with many more vegetables that he could ever use. Neighborhood tradition was always that Mr. Vanzetti would present you with brown paper bags of tomatoes, cucumbers, green beans, squash. Pumpkins for Halloween and pie, watermelons throughout the summer. Toward the end but before the fire he still left vegetables, but no longer bothered to knock on the door and greet you; random bags were found abandoned on the back porch steps from time to time. This was the way of things.

My old man always despised Mr. Vanzetti, for no particular reason, I assumed. The old man was indiscriminate with his hatred, viewing the world with a presumption of treachery, giving everyone he met the benefit of his prejudice and hostility. Then came the day I realized I was wrong, wrong all along; my secret was his secret. The old man and I were brothers in blood after all. My old man knew, knew even before I did, and if he thought I was the one who was going to change anything, he was wrong. He betrayed the world, and so did I; by doing that we couldn't help but betray each other. As for what we did to ourselves, we were both condemned by the silence. Even the fire couldn't burn us free. . . .

Chapter 11

"A joke?" Melissa snatched back the note and stared at the piece of paper. The truth was right here, why couldn't they see it? Why couldn't they see the tears behind her eyes? Did they think they were false? "This is real!"

"I don't think so."

Melissa was chewing on her bottom lip so hard it was a wonder it wasn't bleeding yet. She tried to keep her voice low. "This is real, and you guys need to tell someone."

"The police? No, thanks, but you go ahead. Another false police report and I think you'll just about be on your way."

"What? To Bannerston? You can't do that."

"You're doing it to yourself, Melissa."

His tone frightened her. "This is real, Mr. Ramirez. Please believe me."

"What I *think,*" said Mr. Ramirez, "is that you're more than a little upset about your friend's accident, and that you've reacted in what this file indicates is typical Melissa Maynard fashion."

Melissa shook her head. "I found this note in my locker. It was in one of my books."

"I'm sure it was. I'm also fairly sure you put it there yourself."

"Please."

"Spare me the excuses."

That was close to the same way Jeanette the Witch cut her off the night before and *that* really made Melissa angry. "I'm not sparing you anything; *listen* to me. People are supposed to listen to other people when they have something to say, aren't they?"

Mr. Ramirez picked up his telephone, punched a button. Someone on the other end answered—the secretary probably—and he said, "Could you send a runner to ask Mr. Elliot to come up here? Tell him it's important. Thank you."

Melissa brushed some hair from her eyes. "What are you doing?"

"I'm doing what you asked. I'm arranging for someone to listen to you."

"I don't want to talk to Mr. Elliot right now."

"That's a rather presumptuous statement on your part, isn't it?"

"I can explain if you give me a chance."

"Wait for Mr. Elliot, so you don't have to tell it twice. Besides, he's sort of your advocate, all of you down there in Intervention. Personally I disagree with the whole program, simply tossing good effort after bad, but never let it be said I pounced on a defenseless young girl."

Melissa rolled her eyes. *Please* . . .

Embarrassed, Melissa was still fuming when Mr. Elliot rapped once and stuck his head in the door. When he saw Melissa sitting there he skipped the question he was obviously about to ask and stepped inside, shutting the door behind him. Mr. Ramirez gestured to a seat and he took it.

"We've had some developments here," Mr. Ramirez said.

Mr. Elliot nodded. "I can see that."

Ramirez explained. "Melissa here is off on another

one of her tangents. The problem is I'm beginning to wonder if maybe she doesn't know a bit more about Holly Edinger's accident than she's said."

"I don't." Melissa blurted this out before she realized it wasn't actually true. All she was trying to do was make it clear she wasn't the one who pushed Holly.

Mr. Elliot was more objective. "Wasn't she in class at the time? Can't that be documented?"

This made Ramirez frown. "Yes, I'm sure, but what I'm saying is I think she knows something, and she's off onto one of her wild stories to cover it up. She's done things like this before. For example, this note . . ."

"Note?"

"Oh, yes." Ramirez smiled now. "Melissa would have us believe the whole world is conspiring against her on this."

"Can I see the note?"

"Certainly." Ramirez handed it over, and Mr. Elliot read it quickly. Melissa felt herself blushing, and that made her mad. *Why?* Because she had gone behind Mr. Elliot to take this to the school authorities? Well, why not? She hadn't promised not to. If Russ did this, if Mr. Elliot wanted to protect Intervention from this disgrace, that was his problem. It occurred to her that it wasn't even Russ he was probably trying to protect, it was himself, his reputation, his program.

If Mr. Elliot was annoyed, too bad. That was his problem, she wasn't going to be embarrassed about it, even if she did feel a little weird. He was probably a creep, anyway.

Creaking back in his chair, Mr. Ramirez said, "I think what we need to do is talk to this girl's parents."

"Oh, come on . . ."

"I don't think that's necessary."

Melissa blinked, looking at Mr. Elliot. He was finished reading the note, and he was sticking up for her, raising a point to Mr. Ramirez. Bailing her out? Or something different?

Why?

For his own reasons probably.

Ramirez wasn't immediately buying. He said, "I think we're crossing some lines here."

Mr. Elliot shook his head. "I have to disagree. What we're probably seeing is how Melissa reacts to the serious accident of a friend. A friend in trouble."

Melissa listened to all of this, annoyed. She was a topic now, she hated that, being discusses as if she wasn't a proper human being, as if she wasn't there with them in the room, listening.

Mr. Elliot addressed that issue. He asked Ramirez if he might have a few minutes alone with Melissa, "Just to discuss all of this, give it an airing. Maybe make some sense of it."

"Make some sense? I doubt that's possible."

"Please."

Ramirez grunted, standing up. "Don't be too long with the office, I've got a lot of paperwork."

Mr. Elliot nodded.

Melissa watched the vice principal leave, resisting the impulse to trip him as he came around his desk, buttoning up his suit jacket. He pulled the door shut behind him.

Mr. Elliot flipped the note back onto Ramirez's desk, and folded his hands across his lap. He took a long breath before even looking up at Melissa. "I thought we talked last night."

"We didn't talk. You talked, I listened."

"You hardly listened."

"I didn't like what I heard."

96

Mr. Elliot nodded. "So you feel you've stumbled across something."

"What?"

"Rumpelstiltskin's name."

Melissa shivered, unsure that she had heard what she thought she had. "What?"

Mr. Elliot looked Melissa directly in the eyes now. *"Rumpelstiltskin.* Something Holly Edinger said to me a little while ago."

Swallowing, Melissa said, "You went to the hospital? You talked to Holly?"

He shrugged. "I went up there, but I didn't get to talk to Holly. She's still unconscious. You got a little lucky yesterday. Or a little unlucky."

Lucky? Unlucky? "When did you talk to Holly?"

"Oh, we chatted a little yesterday. On the stairwell."

"You saw Holly on the stairs?"

Mr. Elliot nodded. He got up and walked behind Mr. Ramirez's desk and settled back in Mr. Ramirez's creaky chair. He placed one palm flat on the desk. "Yes, I saw her. We chatted some. Maybe I gave her a little nudge."

Holly? Oh my God . . .

Melissa swallowed. Felt her hands balling into fists, the knuckles white. "A little nudge."

"Well, you know."

Melissa felt her breath stop. A beat. A pause.

No . . .

Melissa's teeth almost chattered, they actually almost did. She shook her head. "I don't know, no."

Mr. Elliot's smile now was almost a leer. "So, do you know Rumpelstiltskin's name yet?"

"I don't care."

"A bit late for that, isn't it?"

Swallowing again, Melissa said, "I . . . I just want to forget all of this."

Nod. Nod. Then a quick shake of the head. "No, that won't do at all. Think about why."

"Please."

"Always polite. I appreciate that. I told Miss Edinger that the notebook was the first draft of a novel, but I'm not sure she believed that. You're all too perceptive, I think."

Melissa tried to think of a good way to get out of this conversation. "Please. I didn't . . ."

"Too late for that."

"Too late for what?"

Mr. Elliot shrugged. " 'The game is afoot.' Or so said Sherlock Holmes. And so say I."

Melissa didn't understand.

"Boo!" Mr. Elliot jumped forward, and so did Melissa. The Intervention instructor laughed. "Bannerston won't be enough, I'm afraid. I think perhaps you'll wind up in a proper mental hospital. We'll see. There's plenty of time."

"Time for what?"

"Things to develop. Life's very complicated, Miss Maynard. There are stranger things in heaven and earth than are dreamt of in your teenage philosophies, Melissa. It's really very sad."

"Sad." Melissa listened to the sound of her voice; it sounded flat, dead.

"The injustice of it all, I mean."

"Injustice?"

"Yes. I just wanted you to understand before any of this actually starts. You're not crazy. *I'm* crazy. I'm the one with things to hide, I realize that. I—"

The office door snapped open, Mr. Ramirez sticking his head inside. Melissa wanted to scream for help, but she didn't. She watched as Ramirez said, "Sorry, I just need a file." He snatched a bundle of papers from his desk and retreated. Mr. Elliot watched him leave and turned back on Melissa, smiling.

She just looked at him. "You are crazy."

Mr. Elliot laughed. "Absolutely. I *am* the one who's crazy. But I sign the reports. I have the power of the hall pass; Russ was correct. Your fate is in my hands, and I'm not going anywhere."

Melissa didn't know what to say.

Mr. Elliot grabbed a pad, scribbling on it as he spoke. "Oh, one more thing." He looked up at her, questioning. "You wouldn't happen to know where Holly stashed my notebook, would you?"

"What?"

"She had it first thing yesterday—I saw it, but I couldn't do anything. By the time I caught up with her, when she had her little accident, well, it seemed to have been misplaced."

"I . . ."

"Pity, too. My mistake, actually. I should have looked before she leaped."

Melissa shuddered.

Mr. Elliot tore the top piece of paper off the pad he was writing on. "Here."

She didn't even look. "What?"

"That's your hall pass, one of my many wielded weapons."

She just looked at him.

Mr. Elliot smiled, shook his head. "You don't want any problems getting into your first morning class, do you?"

Melissa swallowed. "You're my first morning class."

He nodded. "Well, I'm an understanding guy. I thought perhaps you might skip me today. The pass will get you into whatever comes next, no problem."

She didn't say anything.

Mr. Elliot's smile disappeared and he pushed his way out of the office.

Nobody was ever going to believe her.

Stop it! Think!

Trying to stay calm, Melissa walked the hall and kneaded her hands together. That was the best way to keep them from shaking. From shuddering. From clawing out at the air in desperation.

Come on, get a grip. Get a grip.

The police. That was obvious, she could call the police, call and tell them that her Intervention counselor was a cold-blooded mass murderer. Get them out to Yail's Lot to dig around for graves. He said there were bodies buried out there, didn't he?

Maybe he was just talking. Holly knew something, though—*knows, knows! She's going to be all right!*—Yail's Lot was what she said when she woke up and saw Melissa standing there with her.

Oh, yeah, that'll go over real well. That would be a fun conversation with the police. Excuse me, I'm a documented practical joker and I'd like to report this grisly murderer and my friend here will back me up, the one who just took a vicious blow to the head.

Right. Thanks.

Melissa figured she'd be lucky if they didn't lock her up after a story like that.

But what else could she do?

Please . . . Melissa shook her head, trying to clear it, trying to think. Come on, what was she supposed to do? What was she supposed to do?

Go to class now? Go down to Intervention? Go to algebra? Not likely. But that was what Elliot was *counting* on her doing—freaking and blowing off all of her obligations. Give the system and Jeanette the Witch an excuse to throw her out of school, maybe into some institution, give another blow to her credibility and then who was ever going to believe her about anything ever again?

Melissa laughed, a crazy kind of laugh. Terrific, forget it, blow it off. Maybe this was it, maybe she really was going crazy. Maybe that was it, maybe Mr. Elliot didn't really say any of those terrible things. Or, worse yet, maybe this was all some twisted form of therapy, maybe it was all part of some pseudo-psychological babble he was running through her head to make her into a normal person.

Normal.

Normal. The word had no meaning.

Stopping at her locker, Melissa leaned back against it, trying to figure out who she was, why she was stuck in all of this. And where was she, what should she do. Who should she call, who could she tell? Nobody was going to believe her. She half-considered running for the hills, just taking off, saving herself from whatever Mr. Elliot might come up with down the road.

That was one possibility. At least if she was gone she couldn't be killed. At least if she was away from here, away from Mr. Elliot, then she wouldn't have to become a victim.

She lifted herself straight and started walking.

She was rounding the hall corner when hands grabbed her. Tight.

Melissa started to scream, but couldn't; all of the air seemed forced from her body. Two arms were wrapped around her from behind, lifting her off her feet, and a voice growled, "I've got you now, girl! I've got you!"

Chapter 12

Pulling free, Melissa turned to swing wildly in defense and didn't stop, even when she saw that it was Russ clawing at her. He was laughing and her slap caught him by surprise. "You jerk!"

He jumped back before she could slap him again, raising his arms in defense. "Hey, chill! What's the problem?"

Melissa shuddered, pushing at him to stay back. "You're the problem. Everybody's the problem. Just keep out of my way."

Russ didn't seem so inclined, he seemed in too good a mood. Very much pumped up, he trailed her down the hall, talking in a low voice so it wouldn't carry through the doors and draw some teacher out to investigate who was prowling the halls when they should be in class. "Where we going? I just came up to snag something out of my locker."

That was a lie, and Melissa called him on it. "Your locker's not up here."

He shrugged. "Well, somebody's locker is. A buddy's."

Melissa couldn't believe what she was hearing. "You're a thief."

"Not me. You must be thinking of some other guy."

"Yeah, right."

"You in trouble?"

"Always."

Russ bounced. "Hey, you got a pass. You can't be in too much trouble."

She hadn't even realized she was still carrying it. Terrific, the hall pass from hell. She balled the paper and tossed it away; Russ watched her do it. "You missed the trash can," he said.

"I wasn't trying to hit the trash can."

"Good. At least that means your aim isn't off."

"Go away."

"I did. I went away up here."

"Away from me would be nice."

"Nah, come on. Cut me a sprout." Russ mugged a smile.

Melissa sighed, then she asked, "Why aren't you in Intervention?"

Russ shrugged. "Elliot bugged out. So did I."

Rolling her eyes, she agreed. "Yeah, tell me about it."

"I would if you'd give me the chance. Where are you going?" Russ could see she was wandering the halls with little inclination of going to class. He looked around, over his shoulder. "Wherever it is, we should move the show along. Most of the hall monitors know me."

She almost smiled at that.

Russ was following along like an anxious puppy, and she did feel a little bad, since he had been her first, second, and last suspect for every bad thing that had happened so far.

She looked back at him. "I'm ditching out. If you want to come with me you can."

He grinned. "Absolutely."

"Stop smiling. It's not like that."

"I never said it was."

"We're not together."

"Gotcha. We're leaving with each other, but we're not together."

"Knock if off, you know what I mean."

"I wish I did."

Russ followed as she left the building. They passed only one hall monitor on the way, and she was at the other end of the building and didn't bother to pursue to see what was going on. Melissa had no books and she took a deep breath as soon as she hit the sidewalk. It was like some of the pressure was off. Some, not all. No relief could be that great.

At first he just followed, but quickly Russ caught up and walked alongside her. "Okay," he said, "I'm ditching school again, my education is going down the tubes. Where am I off to?"

Melissa answered. "I'm going up to the hospital to see Holly."

Russ nodded, suddenly quiet. "Okay."

"I need to talk to somebody."

He nodded again. "So you're going to talk to Holly?"

"Maybe. I'd like to talk to you."

Another nod, third in a series. "Okay. So how is she? Holly, I mean?"

"Not good. Not much good. She's hurt bad, and that's what I want to talk about."

"Okay."

"Mr. Elliot pushed her over the railing."

If she thought it was impossible to shock Russ, she was wrong. Her slaps had produced nothing like the look on his face now. "Ex-squeeze me?"

"Mr. Elliot is crazy."

Russ nodded, slowly, very slowly. "Doesn't surprise me any, but you need to prove something like that, I think."

Melissa looked up and down the street, choosing

her direction. Then she said, "I'm serious. He confessed it."

"He did?"

"To me. In Ramirez's office."

"He said he pushed Holly over the railing."

"He bragged about it."

"And Ramirez heard this too?"

"No, he was gone then. Mr. Elliot was supposed to be calming me down."

"You don't seem very calm to me."

"I'm not calm at all."

Russ took a long breath. Then he asked, "What exactly are you talking about? Why would Elliot do something like that?"

"Because . . ." Melissa let her voice trail off, then she took a deep breath. "Listen to me very carefully."

"I am."

"Mr. Elliot is stone-cold crazy."

"Okay. What if he is? What are we supposed to do about it?"

Melissa shook her head, not even knowing where to begin. "Do you have a car?"

Russ grimaced. "Car's not the issue, I don't have a driver's license."

This surprised her. "How can a motorhead like you not have a driver's license?"

Russ was very defensive. "Sorry."

"You always told us about your car problems."

"I had one, but I lost it, okay? No big deal."

"How did you lose it?"

"I had an accident. I drove through the back of the garage. Nobody got killed, so let's forget it, okay?"

This almost made Melissa laugh. "You're a lousy driver. You're a big macho guy motorhead and you can't even get out of your garage without wracking up."

"Okay, so maybe you'd be better off finding your old buddy Curt."

"He's not my old buddy."

"He wishes he was."

"Just drop it."

"You drop it too."

"I *am* dropping it. I'm just trying to figure out how to get to the hospital."

A little embarrassed, Russ made a suggestion. "We could take the bus."

"What?"

"I ride the bus a lot, okay? If you want to go to U.M.C., we can get there on the bus easy enough."

"Fine." File this one away for later reference, she thought. This was really weird, learning something this odd about somebody you never pegged like this. Russ was a walking bus schedule.

They went to a nearby corner and had to wait a few minutes, but eventually the number 41 bus came by, just as Russ predicted. "Every half hour," he explained. As they rode downtown they talked. "Suppose you're right," he said, turning from the window to face Melissa; she was sitting on the aisle. "Why wouldn't Holly just rat him out?"

Shrugging, Melissa said, "She only woke up once, so far as I know. I was there."

"Oh. And that's when she fingered Elliot for you?"

"No. She never did. She talked about this place Yail's Lot, though, and so did Elliot and this note I got . . ."

Now Russ looked surprised. "Yail's Lot?"

"Yeah. You know about it?"

"Sure," answered Russ. "That's where the bodies are buried . . ."

Melissa jumped all over him for that one, but they changed buses and were watching for the hospital stop before he even tried to get into it. "You know about the Vanzetti," he said. "That whole neighborhood. I live over there. It's a rat's nest, nobody cares about anything."

"Not even you?"

"Especially not me. I'm just waiting to get out. If it wasn't for my sisters I'd have left a long time ago. My old man's no prize, that's for sure."

"So what about Yail's Lot?"

"It's not so hard to figure. Years ago this rich guy Vanzetti—I guess his name was Yail—he owned the biggest house in the neighborhood, and he had the biggest family. And one by one they disappeared."

"Disappeared?"

"Vanished. First the guy's kids—there were four of them—then his live-in in-laws, then his wife. At first nobody really caught on, then a few got suspicious, but the cops couldn't prove anything. What were they supposed to do?"

"Wow."

"Then the guy's house burned down—with him in it. And that was that. Except—and here's the spooky part—it's like that *wasn't* that. Because once the Vanzetti house was gone—and now practically that whole block is just a field, just the one house there—it's like the house died and helped kill the whole neighborhood. Like a dead spot in the garden, where nothing wants to grow anymore."

Russ nodded, kicking back in his seat. "That's the Vanzetti, just a big black hole in the cosmos, right in the middle of the old neighborhood. Yail's Lot. They never rebuilt there, and probably nobody ever will. We used to walk around and stare at it at night, me and my buddies, but we never cut across. Because it's like an old Indian graveyard or something. It's like it's cursed."

Melissa chewed on her lip a minute. Then she said, "I guess Mr. Elliot knows that story too."

Russ laughed. "Sure he does. That one ratty-looking house still standing on the same block as Yail's Lot? That's where he lives . . ."

They got off at the corner bus stop, and Melissa could see the parking lot where Mr. Elliot had parked when he drove her down. They had to go up into the hospital this time, find out what room Holly was in, so they crossed toward the main entrance. Russ was still talking. "I always figured Elliot for a loon, anybody who wanted to live in a dump on Yail's Lot, but that was just kid stuff. You really think he's crazy?"

"Yeah."

"So why don't we call the cops?"

Melissa rolled her eyes. "Oh, yeah. They'd really believe us, a couple of freaky kids out of Intervention with absolutely no credibility at all."

"Hey, hold up."

"Hold up, what?"

They were at the door now, and Russ explained. "Uh, I'm not real big on hospitals."

"So?"

"So that means I hate to even go inside one."

Melissa rolled her eyes. "What are you doing? Flaking out on me?"

"No, probably I'll just wait outside for you."

"What? Out in the parking lot?"

"Nah," said Russ. He gestured over at a stone bench. "It's not a bad day. No bad cold winds or anything, maybe I'll just sit in the sun for a while."

"There is no sun, just clouds."

"Yeah, but I really can't stand hospitals. Really."

Things were too serious right now for Melissa to even waste time on this, and she told him so. Russ

108

raised both hands, agreeing. "Go on, see Holly. If she's awake or something, I don't know, I . . ."

Melissa listened to Russ not finish another sentence, shook her head, and pushed into the hospital lobby. There was a big desk with a sign above that read VISITORS PLEASE CHECK IN, and she did. The girl there was younger and much more friendly than the nurse at the emergency room had been before, and she said, "Well, it's not really visiting hours, but . . ." She punched Holly's name into the computer, and came up with a room number. "She's still in ICU."

"Intensive care?"

"Yes. They really don't allow visitors."

Melissa swallowed. "I just want to look at her, make sure she's all right."

"Well . . ." The girl considered this, seeming to take pity on Melissa. "You can go up and check with the nurse's station, I guess. It's really up to them, or whatever the doctor says. Fourth floor."

"Thanks." Melissa walked over to the elevators and waited, climbing aboard at the chime when the doors opened and pushing four. She was the only one on the elevator.

When the doors opened again she was surprised to see that the big nurse's station was abandoned. A small color TV was on in the corner, tuned to a soap opera Melissa didn't recognize. There were three empty chairs behind the counter, where a number of electronic devices were monitored.

What was going on here?

Stepping off the elevator, she looked around. She didn't call out—she wasn't real sure she wanted the attention—but she did keep an eye out for somebody, anybody, and nobody appeared.

What was going on?

She passed by the nurse's station, creeping down

the hallway, reading the name slips on doors. The air smelled strongly of antiseptic and cleaning fluids, making Melissa's nose twitch. She kept passing rooms, looking for Holly's name.

She finally found it, room 479. Holly didn't have a roommate; at least nobody else was listed on the door plate, the second slot was empty. Melissa pushed the big door open, walking into the room.

What she saw made her want to break down and cry.

If anything, Holly looked worse than she had down in the emergency room when they brought her in. The tubes were all still in place, and there was a mask over her face, and the placement of all the equipment around her made her look smaller, weaker, more gray in color. Her hair was matted back and in need of washing.

Looking across at her, Melissa felt the strength sapped from her body, and in a moment of longing she felt lonely. Very lonely. And she felt as if she must have forgotten to do something, something much earlier, something Holly must have wanted her to do.

What?

That was when Holly's body jumped.

Melissa couldn't help an automatic smile, out of joy or excitement. Holly! She took a step forward and whispered her name, saying, "Holly, are you all right . . ."

She jumped again in the bed, twitching, and that was when Melissa realized Holly wasn't waking up, she was having some sort of convulsion, as if she were choking.

She *was* choking.

That was when Melissa went into a panic because she didn't know what to do, but she knew she had to do something. There was a mask over Holly's face, and it seemed like there was air coming out, but she was fighting to breathe. Why?

Should she take off the mask? No, she should run for a nurse, but that wasn't right. By the time she got back with somebody Holly could be dead.

Melissa acted. After ringing the nurse's station a few times on the hanging buzzer she started pulling the things off of Holly's face, the tubes looked clogged up, but the stuff was secured down and it took some effort to get it free and it wasn't easy to do and—

"Hey!"

Melissa jumped, startled. In the doorway was Mr. Edinger—*Eddie*—Holly's father, a big guy, along with Holly's mom, whom Melissa knew even better. Melissa called her Toni, and Toni, just like Holly, insisted on calling her "Mo." They were a wildly matched set, Holly and Toni, and a lot of times it seemed like Mr. Edinger—Eddie—was thrown in just to keep order. Now they were there, Eddie and Toni, and not only did they look as if they hadn't slept at all, but they looked more than a little surprised to see Melissa there.

"What the hell are you doing?"

Melissa stumbled over her words. "Trying to help. You've got to get somebody."

Toni set down the coffee cup she was carrying and took off into the hall, but Eddie rushed in and pushed Melissa roughly out of the way. He sounded hoarse. "What have you done?"

"I didn't do anything," said Melissa, still scared for her friend. It suddenly occurred to her that this probably didn't look very good. She found out this was true a second later, because she started to step forward again, just to try to help, but Eddie glared, holding up a hand. "Don't you touch her, or I swear to God I'll knock you through that window."

Eyes wide, Melissa couldn't believe what she was

hearing. This was Eddie, Holly's dad, a guy she knew well, she'd stayed over at Holly's house so many times. Eddie bought them pizza, drove them places, to the movies and the mall, and now he was all fear, all hatred, and a thin black-haired nurse was there now, helping, and Melissa couldn't believe what Eddie was saying to her, because he was saying, "I think this girl did something to Holly, did something to choke her, I think this girl might be the one who pushed her over the railing . . ."

Chapter 13

No. Melissa looked around, in a panic, watching as the nurse and Eddie worked above Holly. Melissa couldn't handle it, couldn't believe what she was seeing. *No.* This wasn't happening. Holly was going to be all right, she was going to be all right.

Toni was back in the room now, standing just inside the doorway. Melissa turned, but Toni wouldn't even look at her.

So Melissa waited, watched. Holly wasn't choking anymore; the nurse had things pretty much in control and motioned for Holly's father to step back out of the way. He did, and Melissa moved. She started to back up, out of the way, but Eddie turned on her again.

"You," he growled. "Don't you even think about going anywhere."

"What?" Even Toni looked confused.

His hands were shaking and he reached for the telephone. It was there on the nightstand and he snatched it up. "I'm calling someone. The police. I want to know what's going on here."

"Nothing's going on here," said Melissa, but she was still backing up, still edging towards the door. "You know me." She looked to Toni for help, for defense, but Holly's mom didn't say anything. *Why not?*

Eddie dialed, waited. "I thought so. I thought I knew you pretty well, but I wonder if maybe your teacher was right." The operator must have picked up now because Eddie spoke to her now, saying, "Get me the police department please. Yeah, the cops; what are you, deaf?"

The police? That was startling enough, but that wasn't what Melissa's first or scariest thought was. This she raised a question she could barely get out: "What teacher?"

"That one of yours. Elliot. Maybe he was right in what he said about you."

"You talked to Mr. Elliot?"

"Yeah, I thought it was all crap. Said I knew you real well. I guess maybe nobody ever knows anybody."

"He went to your house."

"I just said that."

The door was open, pushed in, and Melissa backed past Toni and braced herself against the edge, fluorescent light from the hall falling across her face. "What did he say about me?"

Eddie didn't answer, but Toni did, swallowing once before she spoke. "He said you might be dangerous, Mo. He said you and Holly were fighting, you got her in some trouble. He said he didn't want to get you in trouble, he said he was trying to help you, but he thought maybe you pushed her."

"I didn't. I swear I didn't."

"We'll see." Eddie was talking to the police now.

"Think about it," said Melissa. She sure was. "If he was so worried, looking to help *me* so much, why would he go to you guys?"

"It was the right thing to do."

This was a road Melissa had been down before,

trying to prove herself innocent when a bunch of people had already decided she was guilty. If she waited around long enough they were bound to just nail her with whatever they wanted, even if she did have every excuse in the world.

Every excuse. That was a funny one, since anything she said was automatically a lie. Waiting for the police might be next to the dumbest thing she ever did in her life, and that was a pretty long list. She decided to get out of there, and get out of there *now*.

Melissa didn't wait for the elevator, she ran straight to the stairs, charging down, her footfalls echoing in the empty-sounding stairwell. When she hit bottom she crossed the lobby fast, not looking back and, surprisingly, Russ was still there, waiting outside on the stone bench. He stood and brushed the hair out of his eyes, starting to ask, "So how is she doing—"

Melissa grabbed his arm. "We've got to get out of here."

"Huh?"

"I'm in trouble."

"You said so."

"I mean worse." She explained what had happened in the room, all the while looking around, waiting for a cop car to appear and men in blue to come chasing after her.

Russ looked more than a little impressed. "You're a wild one, aren't you?"

Melissa was walking. "No, I'm not."

He shook his head. "Yeah, well, that's your story. What's keeping me from wondering if maybe you're the crazy one? Maybe you really are the one who pushed Holly. Maybe you did it and don't remember, maybe you just don't know you did it."

"I was in class."

Russ smiled. "Yeah, I know. I was waiting for you

115

to come out. I just wondered what you'd say to that. The cops are gonna ask, you know.''

"I was in class," she said again.

"So why are you running?"

Melissa didn't answer that. Instead she picked up the pace of her walk and sort of changed the subject. They were at least out of sight of the hospital now, moving into the regular downtown now, amongst a lot of stores, many of them out of business, changing hands, or on the way. Dodging cars and crosswalk lights, she said, "You always talk about sticking up for your sisters, but never your brother. I know you've got one; how come you never talk about him?"

"How come you never talk about anybody? Anybody but me, I mean?"

Melissa almost blushed, but she was too distracted, no time for embarrassment. "I asked you first."

Russ shrugged. "My brother's a psycho, doesn't make for much of a conversation. He's in Florida. I hope he stays there."

"Did your dad send him there?"

"The old man? Hell no, he lives for Ryan's nonsense—that's my brother, Ryan. Says he's got high spirits, but that's just another way of saying he's a criminal."

Melissa was surprised and she said so. "The way you are I figured your brother would be your hero or something."

"Or something. However I am, this is the way my brother left me. He ran out. Let him stay gone."

Ran out. That was something Melissa could understand, running. And being left behind. Running was probably better.

Hurt less, anyway.

Russ spoke up. "I hate to be the one to say this, but we should try the cops. I mean, if things are really this weird, why not?"

"Why not?" Rolling her eyes, Melissa said, "Because nobody's going to believe me, that's why not. Nobody ever believes me." She thought about that and corrected herself. "No, that's not true. One person always believes me. One person never calls me a liar. You know who that is?"

Russ didn't.

"Mr. Elliot," she said. "Mr. Elliot the crazy man always believed in me." She gave that a long moment's thought. "But we can't exactly go to him, can we?"

In a way, they did go to Mr. Elliot. They went to him by way of the city library.

The library was a great place to hide out, anyway. A couple of kids didn't have to explain why they weren't in school if they were prowling around aisles full of books.

"Want to explain to me again why we're here?" said Russ. He had always used the library at school as an escape from class, but since they were ditching anyway, he didn't see the point of being here and he said so. He kept saying so.

"I want to know more about this Yail's Lot thing. The Vanzetti."

"I doubt if there's going to be a book on the subject."

"Newspapers," Melissa sighed. "We're going to check back in old newspapers."

"Good luck. I know the old story, but I don't know when any of that stuff happened."

"Maybe somebody will."

They checked with the reference librarian, keeping the questions vague, just wondering how they might find some old newspaper articles. She showed them to a microfiche viewing machine, beside which was a file cabinet in which back issues of the newspaper, the *News-Dispatch*, were maintained. The newspaper went back to 1911, and Melissa still had no idea of where to start.

Russ wasn't about to mess with it. "I'm going to go find a chair in a corner and take a nap."

"I need you."

"That's interesting."

"You know what I mean."

"I can't help you."

Melissa was frustrated. "I can't sit here and read every newspaper, looking for something I don't even know what it is."

"Thank you; I told you that already."

"There's got to be a way to narrow this down some."

Russ shrugged. "Great. Go for it."

There was a computer with a data-base reference index in the library, just across the room, but Melissa had no idea how to use it and she wasn't sure how to go about asking for help on a project like this. It wasn't exactly legitimate, was it?

Leaving Russ to watch the microfiche machine, Melissa went over to the computer and looked for some sort of instructions. There was a tattered white booklet, hardly much use. Who could make head or tail of it?

The computer was on, though. The cursor was blinking beside the heading SUBJECT:

She typed in VANZETTI.

The screen changed, finally coming up with about forty entries. No, forty-*three* entries; at least that's what the total at the top of the screen indicated.

Process of elimination. Melissa simply narrowed the list down to those from town, local at least. All she needed was the dates. Most didn't seem to apply, but there was one that sort of jumped out at her, from the middle 1960's. September, 1965.

She went back to the microfiche machine. Russ was goofing around, holding microfiche sheets up to the light, trying to read the tiny print like a doctor reads an X ray in a hospital movie. Melissa shook her head and he put it back in the box. It wasn't the one she was looking for anyway.

Switching the machine on, she found the film box with the month she wanted and started going through sheets in the machine, which illuminated the newspaper pages like X rays. Russ, of course, couldn't resist a crack. "This thing sounds like an electric razor; I thought libraries were supposed to be quiet. Hey, I'm *not* going to pay a lot to put a muffler on this thing. Ooh, *nice.*"

Another wise guy remark, since the first page she loaded appeared on screen upside down, and she had to try again. "Hold it down," she said when she finally got it to work, adjusting the focus where needed with the knob under the screen. All the pictures and ads looked as if they were straight out of a science fiction movie; seeing the old products and fashions would have been funny any other time. Right now she was in a hurry.

The pages flickered by, Melissa working the controls, pausing only long enough to catch the headlines, get an idea of where she was in time. The St. Louis Gateway Arch was just finishing construction. Watts was burning, fresh from race riots in Los Angeles. The Johnson administration just created a new government agency, the Department of Housing and Urban Development.

Distraction, none of them important.

As the pages flickered by, though, it occurred to Melissa what she was really doing because, come on, seriously, what did any of this mean? Did she really, in her wildest dreams, think that she was going to

119

find something in these old newspapers to justify herself? To make people believe her?

All she was doing was trying to find out Rumpelstiltskin's name, and that was never going to work, not in a million years. Because if Mr. Elliot was that troll, then he was off in his own world, the one he had well in his grasp, well under control. And he was spinning straw into gold.

Straw into gold.

Gold.

There. Melissa frowned, not really believing at first that she was seeing it. September 24, 1965, the local page. BLAZE DESTROYS HOME, KILLS ONE. It was a story about the fire that destroyed Yail Vanzetti's house. The pictures showed two large Victorian houses, alongside each other. One had been completely gutted by the flames. Melissa read the article. Four paragraphs down it said the fire was reported by a neighbor, Anthony Elliot.

Mr. Elliot's father.

Further down the article said arson was the suspected cause of the fire, but Melissa flipped through some more newspapers, a couple of weeks' worth. It took half an hour but there was nothing else about arson burning down the Vanzetti house. It was like they just let it drop.

Let what drop? Melissa had an idea, just as crazy as anything else, probably, but it also made as much sense. And it made her think, wonder. Were the Elliots—Mr. Elliot's father, this time—spinning straw into gold even then?

What happened?

What happened?

I always thought Mr. Vanzetti longed for children of his own, a daughter probably, because he talked often with my sister Rachel, and one time he even gave her a tree to plant in the yard. The tree is dying now, rotted, the roots upending the front sidewalk and damaging the house, and whenever I see it I remember the day I hurt Rachel, the day she and Mr. Vanzetti stopped being friends.

It was a Saturday afternoon, and Mr. Vanzetti had a rabbit in a cardboard box, white and fluffy, a pet, and he was showing it to a group of kids gathered around the back of his car. I squeezed in for a peek and a pet. The rabbit's fur was soft and dry. Rachel wasn't home then, but I couldn't wait to tell her, to show her, and later that day I brought her with me and we went inside the fence and knocked on the door. Mr. Vanzetti answered and I stood strong, asking if we could see the rabbit.

Mr. Vanzetti started laughing, a genuine, affectionate laugh, but there was something odd about it all the same. He called out to his wife, and led us both into the house. "The neighbor kids want to see the rabbit."

He took us into the kitchen, and there he popped open the oven, exposing his roasting dinner. Rachel got sick, gagged then choked, running from the house, and I followed, afraid to be left behind. Mr. Vanzetti's laugh was the last sound I heard from inside of his house for almost six years, until the night he howled, the night we burned him out . . .

Chapter 14

All in all, the few answers Melissa came up with at the library solved nothing. Not really. She was wandering around, Russ tagging along, and Mr. Elliot was still out there, like some weird force of nature, just *out there* somewhere, checking her every move with one of her own.

So the Vanzetti house burned down, killing Mr. Vanzetti, the last of his family. So what. That wasn't exactly news. The idea that Mr. Elliot owned the only house on Yail's Lot was hardly much better. If Holly didn't wake up soon and explain what she meant by what she said about Yail's Lot, then they would never know what the point was anyway.

Mr. Elliot knew something, though. That's why he pushed Holly, that's why he was tormenting Melissa.

A horrible thought pierced right through her: What if Holly never woke up?

Another horrible thought occurred to Melissa: What if Mr. Elliot had no plans to actually hurt her, what if the idea was to just drive her crazy? Honestly, for real, *crazy*.

It was nearly five o'clock and her stomach was tight, hungry, and she was getting in more trouble by the minute. Jeanette the Witch must be loving this, she thought. Oh, yeah, she must be eating this up with a spoon. Melissa the flake, Melissa the nut, Melissa the runaway.

"I need to go home," she said.

"I don't know how smart that is. If you're in trouble they'll just be waiting there for you."

Melissa knew that, but she said, "Either way, I need to know. And I can't wander around forever, for no reason." She gave off a deep sigh, admitting an obvious truth. "I have absolutely no idea what to do next."

Russ, walking alongside her, had an idea. "One thing springs to mind."

"Your mind? This should be good."

"Find some evidence." He stepped around to walk backwards, facing her as he talked. "Let's take a look at Yail's Lot. Probably nobody's ever really done that. If there's something weird there, that would help you prove things."

"Something weird?"

"Yeah, well. You know."

"Like what?"

Rolling his eyes, Russ said, "Okay, bodies or something. That's the old story, isn't it?"

"You think they're just lying around over there?"

"No, but there might be *something*. I don't know what, you said there might be something about Janie, the girl from your class. That couldn't be that long ago."

A thought occurred to Melissa. "This is all just some big adventure to you, some weird quest, isn't it?"

Russ shrugged. "My whole life's a strange game."

"Yeah, well, mine isn't."

"Give it a chance, you might relax. Enjoy things more."

"Oh, yeah, death, murder. A good time to be had by all."

"Got any better ideas?"

Melissa had to admit that she didn't have any ideas at all, good or bad. She also got the idea that Russ didn't really believe what she was telling him about all of this, but in his mind it didn't matter. Any story she might make up was preferable to whatever reality the Powers That Be would lay down on them. Russ was a rebel, and to be a rebel meant you had to rebel sometimes.

Either way, Russ took the idea and ran with it. "Good. So you go home, get in as good as you can, then we'll meet tonight."

"Tonight?"

"It's got to be tonight, we've got to get a handle on this thing."

"I don't know . . ."

"Tonight. Figure ten o'clock. I'll get out and we'll go over there, take a look around."

Melissa nodded. Why not? Most of her bridges were already burned, why not torch a few more. "Okay. Where do we meet?"

"Good question." He considered this, then came up with an answer. "How about right here?"

"Here?" They were at the mailbox at the corner of Eastman and Bruce. Melissa hadn't been totally aware of it, but she was at least wandering in the direction of home. The sun was setting and the street-lamps were flickering on.

Melissa agreed with another nod. "Okay, here."

Russ was pumped. "You sure you can get out?"

"I'll get out."

"Can I call you?"

The notion surprised Melissa. "I don't think that's so bright an idea."

"Can I at least have your number?"

"Why do you need my number if I don't want you calling?"

He smiled. "Well, you know. In case something comes up."

"Forget about it. I'll get out at ten."

"Right."

Raising one finger in a victory salute, Russ twisted on his heels and started to walk away. Melissa had to wonder, what was he so happy about?

Nothing good could possible come of this.

When Melissa got home, the situation fell apart almost immediately. For one thing, Dad was up and about early, which couldn't be a good sign. She had a minute's reprieve, though, because they were both upstairs when she came in, so she at least had a chance to call the hospital, check on Holly. No change. She had barely hung up the telephone when Dad came down, Jeanette the Witch trailing after him. Neither said anything until after they came into the living room, but the way they didn't speak was totally different. Dad was quiet, but looked confused, as if all he needed right now was to be reassured. An explanation might do the trick. Jeanette was the silent victor.

Look at her, Melissa thought, bitter. Just look at her. Happy as a toad in her private little pond.

Irritation and anger weren't going to get her anywhere, though, so Melissa tried to start the conversation. She said, "I've got to talk to you about Mr. Elliot."

Jeanette shook her head, walking right past her to settle on the couch. "The talking is just about over, Melissa. We don't have any choice."

"Choice? Aren't you even listening to me?"

"The school called. You skipped school again, you're telling stories and God knows what else."

"Nothing else. I mean, there's nothing going on." Melissa tried ignoring Jeanette, talking directly and only to her father. "I need to talk to you."

Dad swallowed, uncomfortable. "Mr. Elliot thinks you might be better off at Bannerston. For a while, anyway. A change of environment."

"Bannerston?" Melissa couldn't believe what she was hearing. "Bannerston's a prison."

Jeanette snorted. "Prison might do you good."

"What?"

"Teach you some things, anyway."

Dad interrupted. "It's not a prison, it's a school, a special school, but Mr. Ramirez and Mr. Elliot say it could really help make things better."

"Better for who? Better for Elliot, *sure.*"

"Baby, please . . ."

"*Baby?* I'm not a baby!" Melissa felt like slugging somebody, and Jeanette would have been a great target. She tried again. "He's who I need to talk to you about—Mr. Elliot. This is all a big plot of his, he's tooling around behind my back just to keep anybody from ratting him out. He's totally crazy."

Jeanette was cold. "Let's not talk about crazy."

Melissa looked at her dad. Her father seemed sad, but he also was on Jeanette's side. Big surprise, he pulled another fold. "This school will do you good, I think. Help you concentrate on straightening things out."

"I *am* straight! Mr. Elliot is crazy! He's the nut, he's *killing* people."

Jeanette picked up the telephone, dialed a number from a notepad.

Melissa had an icy thought. "Who are you calling? What are you doing?"

Jeanette said, "I'm calling Mr. Elliot. You're so upset about all this . . ."

"Hang up." Jumping up, Melissa found herself hovering over Jeanette and the phone, looking to Dad for help but seeing none.

"I will not. I'm going to ask if he can come over."

"Oh my God."

Melissa felt sick. She grabbed for her head and started to sit down, but then a burst of panic grabbed her. If she sat down, she was dead.

Dead or worse. What came after Bannerston, she wondered? If Intervention was the last stop before they kicked you out of the world, what did Bannerston represent? A pit stop on the road to the funny farm? Some hospital or asylum?

She pictured Mr. Elliot and Jeanette, co-conspirators in the same crime even though Jeanette may or may not have really known what she was doing. Her act made as much sense as anything else. Adults ran the world, a world full of AIDS, nuclear weapons, hunger, war, ozone-layer depletions, global warming, an endless supply of madness.

Accusing adults—any adult—of being crazy was probably redundant. Maybe just being an adult and having to face the reality of what life really was made you crazy. Maybe Mr. Elliot just represented a different kind of crazy. Maybe the way he twisted truth to his advantage, the way he spun straw into gold, maybe that was just his way of dealing with things, making his life work.

And murder? Well, maybe murder was just grease for the wheels.

Melissa shuddered; too many weird thoughts. Was she starting to slip away herself?

Why wouldn't anyone believe her?

"Where are you going?" Melissa was leaving the room and Jeanette spoke right away.

"For some water." Melissa went into the kitchen and actually did pull down a glass and start the tap. Then she thought, forget about the water, kid, *you're drowning*.

She got out of there.

Chapter 15

Very nervous, Melissa walked alone. Homeless but safe, she thought, or at least as safe as anyone was in this weird world. She might get mugged but she wasn't likely to be murdered by any of her school-teachers, or get shipped off to some institution for Kids Who Couldn't Make It.

At least not tonight.

Terrific.

Walking in darkness wasn't something Melissa was particularly used to, not real darkness. She had to admit the truth, usually she was home before sunset. Now it was after nine-thirty, and she was prowling some strange neighborhood. The Vanzetti, the big boogeyman neighborhood. Was Mr. Elliot the boogeyman?

No. Mr. Elliot was Rumpelstiltskin.

In a way, the darkness seemed to knock away years, things were brighter in the black, younger. Melissa even felt younger herself, not just aimlessly drifting but following a pack of kids home from school. She felt little again.

If only things were that easy to repair. A late-evening wash away of time, another chance to do things, to avoid the mistakes, to make the correct decisions this time. Change, be another person, someone different.

Raising her bag to see if she had a brush with her, Melissa caught her hand in the glow of a street light and saw her nails. Trashed, scratched, and chipped. Wonderful. At least none of them were broken.

Melissa shook her head; what was she, nuts? Life and death were at stake and now she was worried about her nails? That must be the Witch's bad influence, it must be—

"Hey!"

Melissa bounced back a step, and Russ jumped out, laughing. The mailbox at Eastman and Bruce and he was there, trying to make her scream, but she wasn't that jumpy. She was beyond that, and just raised a hand and said, "Don't you ever just say hello?"

Russ shrugged, stepping from the shadows. "Never ease in when you can jump in, never fade away when you can burn out like a match."

"Right."

"Come on, I want to show you something."

"What?"

"Just trust me."

"Trust you?" Melissa laughed, a sarcastic laugh, but she followed him, wondering what was up. They headed toward the Vanzetti, away from the lights, and without even meaning to she found herself stepping closer to Russ, feeling just a bit safer by brushing into him every once in a while as they walked.

"What do you think?" asked Russ after a while. "Was Janie stupid enough to go out on nights like these?"

Melissa shrugged, looking at him. "I don't know, I hardly knew Janie."

"I did. She was a wild girl. Elliot's pet."

Melissa remembered that part. "Yeah." Was that

how the whole thing started? Russ asked, "Do you really think he killed her?"

"He said he did."

"Yeah, but . . ."

Melissa waited.

Russ shrugged. "What I mean is, you don't just kill somebody. Do you think maybe something happened between them? A boy-girl thing, maybe, or what?"

"How would I know? I think he's just crazy."

"Crazy isn't a medical term."

"How about nuts?"

"No. There was probably a reason or . . ."

"What?" Melissa waited, but Russ didn't finish the sentence. He seemed distracted. "What's with you?" she asked.

"You. You're with me."

Russ was smiling, but Melissa shook her head. "We're working together on something, that's all, buddy."

"Right. I'm just saying maybe you don't see the big picture here. Like my brother, he never saw the big picture. My dad, he's a bozo and he drinks and busts things up, and Ryan—my brother—he thought the deal was to break away, run off. But the thing to do is confront."

"Confront?"

"Like what you want to do. Look the evil right in the eye and spit. Like me and the old man. Elliot's not all wrong, you know. A lot of that Intervention stuff makes sense if you think about it, and if he's right there, why wouldn't he be a little right out here in the cold, cruel world?"

"What's any of that got to do with murder?"

"I don't know," Russ shrugged. "There's always a big picture. What do you think?"

Melissa stared, then she said, "What I think is you're starting to scare me."

"Maybe." Russ nodded. "If you saw a snake you would kill it, right?"

The question gave her the creeps. "And?"

"So maybe the main thing is identifying snakes."

Melissa's voice was cold. "He killed Janie."

"Maybe she had it coming."

"Yeah? So what about Holly?"

"You started that one, not him."

"What?" Melissa stopped walking and stepped back from Russ. "Why are you all of a sudden sticking up for a guy who kills people?"

"I'm not," said Russ, raising his hands. "I'm just trying to think this out real slowly. I think you should, too, before we run around screaming killer."

"You said you were going to help me find some evidence tonight."

"I will. It'll be in the lot. Yail's Lot."

"Where the bodies are buried."

"That's the old story."

They walked on and Melissa considered this. "If the story is so old, how come I never heard about it?"

"Well," said Russ, "I think maybe it's one of those stories that floats in certain circles."

The house was up ahead now, lights across the lot, and they walked, skirting it. Looking around, not knowing what they were supposed to be looking for, Melissa figured. Russ kicked at the ground. "I guess I should be honest," he said finally.

Melissa looked at him. "What do you mean, honest?"

"I mean, I like you. A lot. I wanted to ask you out a couple of times, but I didn't."

"So you're asking me on a date now?" This was incredible.

"No." Russ shook his head. "It's just I went to see Elliot."

"You went to see him?"

"I had to."

"And he talked to you? About this stuff?" Melissa felt a chill.

"Sort of," admitted Russ. "I've got my own problems too. It's just there's things."

"Things?"

Russ stood silent a minute and stared around, looking out at the dark. Finally he said, "My brother's not in Florida. My old man killed him."

"Killed him? You mean as in dead?" Melissa felt the whole world start to swirl around her, murder and madness, everything out of control. Was this all she had to face now?

"Yeah," Russ nodded. "The old man killed him, and I knew about it."

"When?"

"Last year. We never told the cops. Whole thing sort of made me crazy myself—that's probably how I wound up in Intervention."

"You didn't tell anybody?"

Russ shook his head, sounding defensive and annoyed. "What was I supposed to do, rat out my own father? He said it was an accident. Maybe it was."

"Oh my God."

"It's okay, though. Because I got the old man. Remember the other day, when I came to school all busted up?"

"Yeah."

Russ leered a bit. "You should have seen the other guy."

"What?"

"I knocked the old man down the stairs. Into the basement. He hit hard, must have busted his neck, he's gone."

"Oh my God."

"But here's what I'm saying, here's why I stay with you, why you need to think about this. Mr. Elliot's only a little crazy, he doesn't run around killing people. Only every once in a while something happens, or somebody really has it coming."

Melissa backed away, fumbling with her purse, trying to force it open.

"Take it easy. Listen, I'm not a monster. The old man was a maniac, he was going to kill somebody else, me or my sisters. So he's gone, so what. Elliot's going to help me take care of the body. It's cool."

"No."

"And it's going to be okay with you. He said he'd back off if you would. Come on, he's got the power of the great and holy hall pass, he can get us both out of psychomania and back up with the real people."

"No."

"Come on, Mo, help me out on this."

"No!" Melissa had her mace out now, the rape mace, only she couldn't remember how to work the stupid trigger on the thing. The Witch showed her a couple of times, but now she couldn't remember.

Still trying, Russ said, "Hey, it's okay."

"No!" Russ moved fast but Melissa sprayed. The shot mostly missed, though some of the mist stung him, forcing him back with a screech.

"We're not like other people, Mo; if we keep straight with the rules they'll screw us over until we die."

"Stay away from me."

"I just want to talk," said Russ, but he was jumping for her and she swiped out with her left hand. Her nails dug into Russ's face and two broke, and there was blood.

Then she fired the mace again and he dropped.

Melissa ran off into the dark.

Chapter 16

This wasn't happening, it wasn't happening. Not this.

He could be dead, she realized. Russ could be blinded and bleeding and dead and she would have done it and she didn't care. She was running, and she wanted to get far away.

Rushing, crossing the lot, Melissa felt hypnotized by the lights of the house on the far corner, lights that twinkled through the branches of the trees and bushes that cluttered the lot, the waist-high grass, and she thought for a second that she could reach out of the shadows, reach up to the moon. Maybe even make herself young again. She could be younger; she was younger, ten years old this time, and maybe she could—

Stumbling, Melissa yelped, cried out. Fell.

The earth opened up and consumed her.

The ground was open and she fell in, but it was only clumps of earth that followed her down into the hole, landing on her. She hit bottom suddenly, her left shin striking something sharp that hurt; she yelled again. It was like falling into a grave.

At first she lay not moving, stunned. Then Melissa realized, with creeping nausea as all of her senses took stock . . . it was a grave.

She panicked, scrambling for escape, clawing at

the earth. She tore at clothing—not her clothing. Rotted black fabric caught in her hands. She couldn't get rid of it, couldn't wipe it away from her. Also she hurt; she had struck her leg on a shovel in the hole with her, a digger's spade, and she thought she might even be bleeding.

Melissa realized she was screaming in her horror, and when hands reached down to help her she grabbed for them desperately, not even thinking about who might be there. "Easy," said the voice, familiar. "Easy. Be quiet."

Melissa was quiet. She was hurt, bleeding, and silent, but her mind was screaming.

What happened next was a blur, part of the shock. The man who pulled her from the pit brought her to a house, took her inside the house, and helped with her leg. There seemed to be blood everywhere, dripping on the rugs, the tile, the bathroom floor, and in the tub, where water was running. Her blood, Melissa's blood, and the pain numbed her leg into nothingness, as if it wasn't even attached to her body.

Her mind was screaming because of what she had seen beneath her as she struggled to get out of the hole . . .

Mr. Elliot was with her, she realized that with a start. It was Mr. Elliot, all the time, washing clean her wound, wrapping it in cloth. Torn sheeting, she thought. Not thick, but tight. Blood quickly soaked the cloth, but did not seep through. It seemed to slow to a stop.

Death . . . death . . . death was in the garden. Melissa saw the face, and the face was . . .

Mr. Elliot eased her back into the living room and brought her a blanket. Melissa wasn't moving, but her teeth were chattering, cold. "Where's your buddy?" he asked.

Melissa didn't answer.

"Russ couldn't make it? Let you out to wander alone?"

Melissa didn't say anything.

Shrugging, Mr. Elliot smiled, a flat smile. False. "He's wondering a lot about you now, I think."

Melissa waited, sick, numb, cold. She didn't know what might come next, and she was in no position to run or to fight.

Mr. Elliot smiled, his lips stretching back together, tight like a mask suddenly strange to him. "You're scared."

"I saw what was out there."

"You mean my transgressions," he murmured.

"Transgressions?" The voice in Melissa's head was only a little quieter now, repeating, like a scratched recording. *Death . . . death . . . death . . .*

"*Transgressions.* Sins. Things we can't take back, can't undo."

"What?" Melissa didn't understand.

Mr. Elliot took a breath, and there was a long moment of silence.

Melissa shook her head to clear it, but she found herself almost stuttering when she spoke, trembling, as if from the cold. "That body. That woman. You killed . . ." Melissa stopped talking then, because she was flashing on the hole again and another horrible thought occurred to her. "Was that Janie? Was it?"

"No." Mr. Elliot shook his head, reassuring her. "No, that wasn't Janie. That was something terrible from a long time ago, and I swear I had nothing to do with it. I didn't harm that woman at all."

Crazy, Melissa was thinking as Mr. Elliot wormed his way through a calm denial. He's totally crazy. She said nothing, though; she didn't know how far she might push before he struck out, did something bad. She was trying to figure a way out of this.

137

Mr. Elliot leaned forward, very intense, very curious. He lifted her hand, touched the broken nails. Then he asked, "How could you tell that the person in the ground was a woman? She's been in the yard for an awful long time."

Melissa tasted the top of her mouth; it was sour. She couldn't shake the smell, either, the horror. She felt a little faint.

No, she thought. Stay together. Don't panic.

Mr. Elliot was thinking. "The clothes perhaps. Well, thank goodness for the clothes. Without the clothes I'd have had a sorry mess indeed to pull together from the garden. The bodies are so decomposed . . ."

Melissa turned away, sick at the thought. Bodies? More than one? How many? Two? Six? A hundred?

"I'm sorry," said Mr. Elliot. "You see, I never intended to recover those graves, not in my lifetime. I was always sure they would be found eventually, someday. That was the reason for the notebooks, to make sure my story was told. I've always kept a diary."

Looking around now, Mr. Elliot said, "But sometimes now I'm not so sure, sometimes my resolve falters and even I feel like running away. What was it Russ always said? I can't just write myself a hall pass into the next world, the better world. Still . . ." He shook his head, searching for his next thought.

Melissa felt herself gagging. *Recover.* The thought of the meaning he was attaching to the word "recover" made her instantly sick. A technical term for a goulish act. She shook her head. "You kill people."

"Only two. But the yard . . ." He stopped, frustrated by something.

"What?"

"The yard is full, but I didn't do it. But the world

will never accept that, they'll say it was me and I . . .''

Melissa watched him work up to the next.

"Janie was my friend," he said. "More than a student. She understood me like no woman ever has. And I thought I understood her. I didn't mean to hurt her.

Hurt her? "Did you kill her?"

It took a moment, but he nodded. He rose and poured himself a cup of tea and, on consideration, added some brandy to it. He held up the bottle in silent offer for another moment but Melissa made no acknowledgment.

There was a knock on the door, slow and steady rapping, and Melissa jumped, scared. Mr. Elliot's eyes jumped right and left, then he slowly stood up and walked to the door. Her heart racing with anticipation, Melissa watched to see, but shuddered. The door opened and was pushed back, and Mr. Elliot stood there with the battered-looking Russ, whom he gestured to one side of the room and told to be quiet for a while.

Knotting her hands together, Melissa wondered if she would die soon. And how?

Mr. Elliot settled back on the couch, ignoring Russ for now and talking about himself. "I loved Janie. I thought she loved me; I think she did. Both of us were split, I thought we could be one person, even though she was much younger and my soul is as if it is hundreds of years old. But she didn't understand, and when she found out about me . . .''

Mr. Elliot looked as if he might start crying. He was genuinely hurting and Melissa could feel it.

He pulled himself together. "What happened with Holly was an accident, almost an accident. I snapped, but I won't snap again. This is going too far, even the thing with Russ.''

Looking toward Russ, who was still standing in the corner, Melissa said, "Now you're both murderers."

Mr. Elliot shook his head. "No, Russ did what he felt he had to do. As we all do." He looked around, shrugging. "So much of this is on me, I've gone too far, and every step of the way I was just trying to keep one foot in my reality. As it is, it's mostly gone."

"It doesn't have to be," said Russ. "We can help each other."

Mr. Elliot shook his head. "It's all right, Russ. We'll do whatever has to be done."

"You were going to help me."

"I will, one way or the other."

"I don't want the other."

"Quiet." Mr. Elliot looked to Melissa. "Well. What comes next? The police? The press?"

Again, Melissa didn't say anything. Not out loud.

"What about your leg? Do you need to go to the hospital? A doctor?"

Melissa just blurted it out. "You guys could just leave, you could both go."

Russ raised his hands to his face in frustration, but Mr. Elliot just seemed amused. "What?"

"Run away. I couldn't stop you."

"There's so much to explain."

"What?"

"I didn't do these things, Melissa. You've got to believe me. I'm not capable of it, not really. That's why I need people not to believe you. But they will; eventually you'll attract someone's attention. So I have to get rid of the bodies—bodies I did not put there. But I couldn't hurt you, not now. Not after all this. If you could have run you would have easily got away outside, because I wouldn't have followed. It never would have occurred to me to follow."

Following another sip of tea, Mr. Elliot said, "Now

140

I'm wondering. Just wondering. I'm not sure I want to be a fugitive. I don't know what to do. I know I didn't kill anybody, but everybody will know I did. Ever hear of Lizzie Borden? Took an ax and gave her mother forty whacks?"

"Yes."

"Well, Lizzie Borden never killed anyone. She was acquitted." Mr. Elliot stared at her a long moment, sipping from his cup. Russ watched too, awaiting some command, it seemed, but not speaking. Was he waiting to help kill her? Melissa shivered, but other than that did nothing. Her inaction seemed to puzzle him. "You don't know what to do."

Very quiet from Melissa: "Maybe not."

"You should be horrified."

"I am."

"No," Mr. Elliot shook his head, looking to Russ and back to Melissa. "That's not enough, you should be *mindless* about this. Terror should have you, you should be running now, stumbling against the door, trying to work the bolts. You should be in the streets, screaming for the police and praying not to die . . ."

Nothing from Melissa.

Now it was Mr. Elliot's turn to shudder. "I'm a *monster,* how can you sit here with me?"

"You said you didn't kill anyone."

"I didn't. But I know who did. I knew when it was happening, or right afterwards, anyway. And I never told anyone."

"What?"

"There's a problem with burying bodies. If you place them too deep, sometimes you forget where you put them, Or why you did it. Bury them too shallow and sometimes they come crawling back . . ."

"What happened?"

"With me, you mean? Funny story. Mr. Vanzetti—Mr. Yail Vanzetti, owner of house and lot—was killing people, including his own family. Burying them in his yard. My father found out about this, stumbled on to it somehow. I discovered the circumstances around that. But, like the good Germans who sat quietly as the smokestacks of Dachau were filled with human beings, my daddy didn't tell anyone."

"Why?"

For the first time, Mr. Elliot glared. "He had his reasons. Of course it was only a matter of time before someone else also found out, and that was me. I was twelve at the time, and there was nothing I could do because I had my father to worry about. And Vanzetti kept filling his garden. Another grave would appear in the lot, and my father would point it out to me and there was nothing I could do.

"I ran away a couple of times, I couldn't deal with it. Daddy kept bringing me back. Finally my father snapped. Anybody would. I helped him, and I thought I was being a hero as I did it. We burned Vanzetti's house down, killed him. Made an end to it. But we had the guilt, we had the lot to deal with. Because he left the house and lot to my father in his will, and my dad left it to me.

"That's the curse, Melissa, the strain. The sin of omission. It's like the story from the Bible. Original sin wasn't disobedience, Melissa. It was false witness. Eve lied about the serpent. She ran away from her troubles, just as I did, just as you do. We're all runaways. Evil, silent runaways, all searching for absolution, looking for that hall pass to make the bad things go away, get us out of trouble. Confrontation is so difficult."

Melissa looked at Russ. He didn't meet her eyes; instead he crossed the room over to the fireplace and lifted a heavy poker, the thing you pushed the coals around with. He seemed caught up in something.

Mr. Elliot sighed. "I should kill you, Melissa. It's

the intelligent thing to do. Perhaps I will, if I can work up to it. If I can't convince you about life, maybe I'll just make your life go away for a while. Or better still, maybe I could give the house and lot to you, just as it was passed to me. Would you like that?''

Russ stood frozen at the fireplace and Mr. Elliot was caught up with his new image. "Yes, just like the Welsh sin-eaters. The Druids could escape hell by passing along their sins to the living. That's sort of what I did for my father and Mr. Vanzetti; I ate their sins. I never told, never spoke until now, and you too could keep the silence, Melissa. You could guard that silence.''

"You want me to be a murderer too?'' The thought terrified her, but at the same time she felt something else. Something even more scary.

"No." Mr. Elliot shook his head. "Keep your own counsel. But always devour those who could subdue you.''

"No.''

"Your stepmother, for example. Is it a right and proper world if she wins, has you put in some hospital?''

Kill the Witch? Murder a person? "No.''

"Guard my silence. I'll help you guard yourself. We'll help you, Melissa.''

Melissa didn't wait. Looking first to Russ, she got up and, on her feet, stumbled away, and it was as if she were slipping down slimy walls into a dark well. Russ was frightened but Mr. Elliot held him back with a finger and a word and Melissa, unable to properly balance or to right herself, saw herself passing through the front door of the house as if viewing the scene through some cloudy mirror. The coolness of the air swept her away with the blowing leaves, red and brown and orange, all black now in the night shadows. The musky smell of dampness and earth from the garden digging grabbed for her, but she made it to the iron gate. Nothing awaited her there save the sidewalk, but she stumbled on.

She went straight for home without stopping.

Chapter 17

Confrontation was difficult, so said Mr. Elliot.

That was true enough. Melissa didn't feel as if she could confront the police—why not? There were bodies in the yard—but she went home ready to confront Dad and Jeanette the Witch.

Only Dad was working, of course, that's right, and Jeanette—although she was up and waiting and cold—had her own little agenda to push. "Thank you for finally making this possible," she said, meeting her in the half-lit living room. "Eventually you'll be grateful."

Melissa didn't understand. "Grateful for what?"

"The new arrangements." Jeanette the Witch handed her a folded colorful paper and went into the kitchen. The expression on her face was nothing less than satisfaction. "After all, you've always wanted to go away. I found you a ticket."

ChapterView Hospital, read the brochure. For dependency problems, depression, and psychological illnesses. A caring place, a people place.

The funny farm.

No way.

"This isn't happening," said Melissa, following her stepmother out into the kitchen. "You don't understand."

"I don't need to understand," said Jeanette. "I don't have to understand."

"So what do you think you're going to do? Just send me away, just like that?"

"Just like that."

"I know things. We need to call the police. Mr. Elliot is a murderer. Russ is a murderer. Everyone is killing people around me."

Jeanette nodded, calm. "Tell that to the doctor at your interview tomorrow. And don't bother getting up to go to school. We have appointments all day."

"What are you talking about?"

"The hospital, getting you out of school, switching things around for your stay."

"No."

"Yes. What have you done to your leg?"

Melissa placed a hand on the bandaged wound. "This is what I'm trying to tell you."

"We'll have that checked out as well. Go to bed."

"Jeanette, please."

"Go to bed."

"I'm begging you."

"Maybe. I'm finished begging you." Jeanette stepped closer and spoke, very serious. "Since we've come this far, let me put my cards out on the table. You're leaving here and I'm glad. I tried my best to adjust to you, to you and your nonsense, and what did I get? Appreciation? No. I got abuse and insult."

"Jeanette . . ." Melissa tried to think of something to say, but nothing came out. Besides, Melissa felt tight and angry now; why should she answer?

"Fair enough," shrugged Jeanette. "You don't love me and I sure don't love you. Just like your mother, aren't you, Miss Melissa? Too good for your father, and too good for me. Well, it's just about good-bye. I'd wish you a happy life, except . . ."

146

Jeanette smiled, a phony smile. "Except I don't wish you one."

Melissa stepped back. Jeanette shook her head, but then a thought occurred to her. "You know, sometimes I thought you were one of those teenage suicide cases, a mixed-up girl who might take her own life. Sometimes I wished you would."

"What?" Melissa trembled, hating the Witch.

Jeanette turned and went upstairs herself and Melissa collapsed on the couch a while, feeling her leg throb and wondering what to do, who to tell, what to answer. She hated Jeanette and for a second actually wished her dead, but then she remembered all the other deaths, and the thought scared her because it came so easily.

Dad would never let this happen. He couldn't. Except sometimes he did.

Melissa didn't remember falling asleep that night, but later the throb of her leg and the sound of digging woke her. Or maybe it was still a dream, maybe it was all a nightmare. She told herself that she didn't want to look down to see, but she did. Busy with their tasks, Mr. Elliot and Russ glanced up in her direction, as if she was the master and they the nervous servants, fearful of being caught inattentive to their work.

Melissa watched from the window, unsure of why she could see Mr. Elliot's yard from there until she found herself with them, beside them, clawing at the mounds of earth with her bare hands while Russ struck ground with a poker and Mr. Elliot worked the spade. They did not speak. Corpses, one after another, came to the surface, stacking up like rotting cordwood beside the vegetable rows. The last body they pulled from the ground had the taunting face of Jeanette the Witch.

Melissa woke up, for real this time, not with a

147

scream but with a small noise, perhaps a whimper. The last image of the dream was still with her, that of an empty garden torn asunder in the morning sunlight. The handle of the shovel stood like a lone crucifix on Golgotha.

Downstairs, Melissa's father was already starting to make his usual mess of things in the kitchen; the sounds were unmistakable. Jeanette was there as well, and the talk was of hospitals, of the best and proper things. Melissa was now simply a topic. Here her leg was throbbing, but the wound didn't seem so bad when you considered what else was happening. Just a burning ache that stabbed, but was tight like a knot, making her gasp as she unbended her leg. In the corner of the room, the clock radio switched on, the sudden unpleasant sting of rock and roll. A musical intrusion from a world Melissa had lost her place in.

No. Melissa steeled herself.

She was going back to Mr. Elliot's house, to talk some more, to learn.

Rumpelstiltskin was his name. Keeper of the hall pass.

Jeanette the Witch made the rules. She wanted to keep the princess, the king's daughter, chained down in some hovel. No way.

Melissa was going to see Mr. Elliot.

It was time to spin some straw into gold.

ROBERT HAWKS is the author of close to a dozen books for young people. He lives in Las Vegas, Nevada, with his wife and their two daughters.

Order Form

To order direct from the publishers, just make a list of the titles you want and fill in the form below:

Name ....

Address ....

....

....

Send to: Dept 6, HarperCollins Publishers Ltd, Westerhill Road, Bishopbriggs, Glasgow G64 2QT.

Please enclose a cheque or postal order to the value of the cover price, plus:

UK & BFPO: Add £1.00 for the first book, and 25p per copy for each addition book ordered.

Overseas and Eire: Add £2.95 service charge. Books will be sent by surface mail but quotes for airmail despatch will be given on request.

A 24-hour telephone ordering service is avail-able to Visa and Access card holders: 041-772 2281